THE REPROBATES

Benjamin Grose

First paperback edition 2022

Book design by PublishingPush

Print ISBN : 978-1-80227-772-2
eBook ISBN : 978-1-80227-773-9

benjamingrose.co.uk

For all the people who remember how it used to be.

You are not the kind of guy who would be at
a place like this at this time of the morning.
But here you are...

—Bright Lights, Big City

You can disappear here without knowing it.

—Less Than Zero

my spirit was long ago
broken
in lonely places.

—Charles Bukowski

I work in a nightclub where the only people more rep-rehensible than the customers are the people serving the drinks. People come here because we're still open when everywhere else shuts, and the drink is cheap because they know someone behind the bar—and even if you don't, you soon will.

Welcome to Munks. The ceiling is sweating. The lights are coming on. The dance floor is illuminated. The bouncers are shouting for everyone to go home. The staff are collecting plastic cups in big green recycling bags. The customers are no longer customers—they're the unwanted, the wasted, the faceless. Some are collapsed on the old red leather sofas. Some are hunched over the round tables, asleep. Some are still dancing, even though the music has stopped. Some want more, they always do—but the big boards are up on the bars, and the only way out of the dungeon is up the stairs and out into the night.

I'm the manager, and I'm responsible for them all.

*

Cashing up—staring into a screen of numbers, trying to make everything fit and restore some balance to a place

1

of moral bankruptcy. A thousand pounds here, a thousand pounds there. I'm ten pounds down on the upstairs bar till, but find it in the door till, use a pound from my pot on the desk to fill a gap, discover we're twenty quid down on downstairs till #2 but find it hiding in the change drawer, then print out the cash sheet on the dodgy printer, put it all in a bag and into the safe below to which only the new owners have a key. I've put hundreds of thousands of pounds in there. Never to be seen again.

There's a knock on my office door. Meet Mike, the head bouncer. He comes in with the doormen's radios to put them on charge for the night, and a couple of Vodka and Cokes that, knowing him, will only have a dribble of Coke in them—it has that muddy water colour with a few bubbles in the bottom and it makes my vision spotted with each sip.

He rubs my back—"Don't worry, sweetness, that's another Saturday night all over."

He's a fifteen-stone skinhead who used to own a gym and has a newborn daughter with his Eastern European wife who used to do the door till here. We're a very close bunch, and the night shifts turn us into strange creatures, the likes of which you won't find on any David Attenborough programme.

*

There are names and dates on the wall of the upstairs bar. The Smiths 83, Oasis 94, Klaxons 06, Blur 90, The Cure

83, the Killers 04, Radiohead 92. Bands play here before they get famous. That's the foundation of Munks' reputation. The other reputation is one the new owners are trying to wipe out—we're infamous for being the place where the customers drink cheap booze until they collapse in their own vomit and are then laughed at by the staff, who are almost as inebriated as they are. The new owners have started the cleansing of this place by making the upstairs bar into a Music Café and making a new daytime entrance. If the rumours are true and they are as mad as they seem, soon they'll be serving food. In a nightclub? you might ask. But no. Officially, this is no longer a nightclub. It is a Live Music Venue that does club nights.

It is a common practice these days apparently—abandoning any reason for madness.

*

Meet the people who are in the business of getting people drunk.

There's Harrison, the closest I have to a best friend—thespian extraordinaire, Jackson—Jeremy, our resident homosexual—Cub, who lives with Jeremy and is currently studying for her second Master's—Bran, who looks like Sideshow Bob, has worked here ten years and at twenty-seven still lives with his mum—Freddy Nelson—Freddy Nelson's girlfriend Leah who got Freddy his job (everyone here has got at least somebody a job)—the dreadlocked Freddy Maytal—Tattoo Paul—Shelly—Laura the Essex girl—and Inez, the Spanish expatriate who has been in this city longer than anyone. ·

They're an eclectic bunch. At least to begin with they are. Then, a week into the job, the drink, the drunks, the twilight hours take over. Their new shoes fall apart thanks to the sticky floors and the grime—scuffed, puked on, full of holes after a few nights of dealing with the juice mob. This place has moulded them into a ragtag bunch of students and ex-students stuck in the same city, band members with a dream of the big time, once upon a time teenagers now in their mid-twenties, then their mid-thirties, always about to get a real job—but all going nowhere except the pub next door on their night off.

I'm as bad as any of them. I've been here eight years, manager for two and a half of those, and I can't remember the last time I left this city.

*

There is no shame in this place. When people walk through those doors, pay their money and receive their stamps, all inhibitions, all concerns, all sense is stripped away. It leaves people like this guy, who is currently urinating in the corner of the dance floor whilst smoking a cigarette. People start to notice, and they stand back, some laughing, some speechless, as the doormen push their way through to him just as he's doing a final shake. He puts his cigarette out in his puddle of piss and turns around, a satisfied, pleasant expression on his face as if he's just decided to go to the bar for another drink. He starts walking in that direction before the bouncers steer him through the fire exit and shut the door behind him.

*

Meet the people who are in the business of throwing the drunks out. Mike, the head bouncer—Stacie, the hairdresser bodybuilder—Sam who has an IQ of 11 or maybe 12 and hands out humbugs to fat girls—Pete Bone, the meanest, most ignorant bastard you will ever meet—Judo Phil—Pete 2, the electrician—Bill, the social recluse and suspected virgin—Slicer, who is only five feet tall but grew up fighting his way through his many cousins in a bare-knuckle boxing ring—and Abasi, the biggest, hardest son of a bitch in the city.

*

In this place, I've watched some of the best bands I've ever seen in my life. I've also seen some of the worst.

Take tonight for example. I'm sitting at the door till, and four people have paid six pounds each to see a band called Upside Down Clinic—a fat woman in a pink dress banging a snare drum and warbling in a language nobody recognises, and a skinny man on a keyboard wearing trousers several sizes too big for him. It is quite possibly the worst thing I have ever heard. I'm preparing myself to go downstairs and find corpses. Not the sound man though.

Jeff has seen worse—he's been here for twenty years and will probably be here another twenty.

When it finally ends, and the four customers come back up the stairs to leave, I turn my gaze to the floor, not wanting to make eye contact in case one of them asks for their money back.

They have a right to.

I blame the new promoter.

*

Meet the new promoter, Dom. A thin, pale kid with a whiny voice and a permanently pinched look on his face. He wears chunky white trainers with wings on. Seriously—big, bulky things with silver wings on the laces. We should start calling him Pegasus. He supports Wigan Athletic, drives a Ford KA and still lives with his parents in the neighbouring city.

Dom—much younger than me, barely twenty-one—the man tasked with bringing this place back to its glory days by the new owners.

I think we have different opinions on when the glory days were.

*

Meet the guy passed out in the left-hand cubicle of the Gents' toilets. Mike, Sam, and I have just found him, collapsed, sitting with his back to the door, what we can see of his jeans wrapped around his ankles, pants down, belt loose, naked arse cheeks on the grimy floor, his boxer shorts so stained and wet it's difficult to tell their original colour. Sam tries to open the door but the guy's jammed between the toilet and the door and the gap isn't wide enough to get in.

"Mate! Wake up!"

Sam and Mike try everything—knocking, knocking louder, throwing water over the top of the door, everything, until finally he mumbles and starts fumbling for something and his belt buckle jangles and scrapes along the tiled floor and he moves a bit and Sam can see all of the way in. He swears and says, "He's fucking shit himself, the dirty bastard."

He hasn't just shit himself, he's pissed and puked on himself too, which we find out when we finally get him to stand up, and he walks out, a dead stare on his face, caked in crap and dirt, a great big globule of toilet roll stuck to his neck. He stands at the sink in front of the mirror, says nothing, and runs the water.

Mike sniggers—"I think he's got more pressing problems than dirty hands."

The guy goes without a fuss, but a few hours later, when I'm leaving after locking up, I walk past him again, collapsed on the steps of a house on the next street. His head is in a polystyrene box of half-eaten chips and there is ketchup and mayonnaise in his hair, and if I didn't know better, it would be a reasonable assumption to think he'd been clubbed to death whilst frantically filling his throat with dregs and dog cuisine from 'Yummys', the local kebab shop.

I stand there for a while, then walk on a few yards. Stop. Go back and sit down next to him on the steps, pull out a cigarette, light it and look at him again. See myself lying there. Then I find my phone and ring a taxi, hoping he'll wake up soon and give me an address.

*

I don't know whether it's just a coincidence, or that the guy who put it there is a pervert, but the cloakroom is opposite the Ladies' toilets. The cloakroom—discounting the manager's office—is perhaps the strangest place in this godforsaken club. Philosophy litters the walls—**DRUGS SEX & TEA—HOMOPHOBICS ARE GAY—COATS ARE FOR TWATS—DON'T EAT CHILDREN**. It is a money-making scheme, a shopper's delight, a place of solitude, desperation, and ill health. Mould is climbing the walls and polluting our lungs. It epitomises this club, and there are ghosts here suffering from an endless hangover.

I sit in the old leather chair, covering for Tattoo Paul whilst he goes for a fag or three. He has clipped out a line from a food and drink magazine, scribbled out the TAIL, drawn an upwards arrow and stuck it to the shelf below the counter so it reads **COCK~~TAIL~~ ↑ OF THE MONTH**. It is currently pointing to a very well-dressed, well-spoken chap holding a memory stick.

"What?" I ask him.

"My parents used to come here," he says.

"Great."

"Can I DJ?"

"Sorry?"

"This DJ is frankly absolute shit. I will double the numbers through the door. I guarantee it." And he thrusts out a hand to shake on it. "I won't even ask for a fee."

I agree with him about the DJ—it is drum and bass night—but I'm shaking my head.

"What are you going to use?"

"This!"

We both look at the memory stick.

"Mate, think about it. I'm not letting you DJ."

He stands back—suddenly aloof, shaking his head, aghast.

"My parents used to come here."

He storms off with his memory stick and his music morals, and I sit back and look down at the words written across the shelf below the counter.

WHY DID I TAKE THIS JOB?

And below that—

BECAUSE YOU FANCY MIKE!

*

Tuesday night is Cheese Night. Students come from all over the city in stupid clothes to drink cheap doubles and get greased up on the sticky dance floor to S Club 7, Total

Eclipse of the Heart, and the Grease Medley. It's thirty deep at the bar and you can't move.

I hide in my office until I feel guilty and go out and give them a hand behind the bar. The tide always breaks at 1:30 am when the great exodus starts and they all beg for water and find somebody, anybody, to sleep with.

A ginger kid wanders through the midst, no shirt on— the words **MY PARENTS ARE COMING TOMORROW** written in pink pen on his stomach.

*

The four most important things I have learnt about this place—

Come 2 am, the Ladies' toilets are always in a worse state than the Gents'.

If you're short of cash then look to the floor at closing time.

Every night brings a new minesweeper.

The customer is always wrong.

*

Meet the new owners. Terry is a small, balding man with friends in high places and a wife equally as high because she is four feet taller than him. His business partner, Karen, is an odd woman who looks like she didn't smoke enough weed as a teenager but tells everyone she smoked too much. I don't know what to make of her, but it's clear that she's the driving force of the partnership, the axe-wielder, the one who's not afraid to chop off heads.

Karen is talking bollocks—droning on and on about the future of Munks.

Terry sits back, says little—a strange, small man with a rough voice.

Dom nods every few seconds and says, "Hmmmm… yes… I agree."

I think agonisingly of what else I could be doing right now. Washing the car. Hoovering the flat. Cleaning the toilet.

The current topic of conversation is the new Friday night they're developing.

"Of course, Dom will come to you soon with all the details…"

"What are you going to call it?"

It's the first thing I've said—they look at me, bewildered, I think more by the fact that after half an hour I've finally said something than by my question itself.

"Erm," says Dom, "we have drawn up a hit list of names."

"Oh yeah… which are?"

He just looks at me.

"Why don't you ask the staff? They can be a creative lot at times."

"Well," Dom looks sideways at Karen, "it's something we'll consider…"

*

This building is old. Nothing works. The sinks are blocked. The drains smell. The toilets are broken. The walls are crumbling. The ceiling is leaking. The cellar is a cold stone hole with muck and rat skeletons behind the barrels, all lined up in a row along the wall. I spend all day there, avoiding the daylight, scrubbing, cleaning the crap and muck away even though I know it's going to come back.

*

I'm standing on the edge of the dance floor when a girl comes up to me and asks if I work here.

"Why?"

"Because there is a man over there who is scaring me and my friends."

I look over. Meet Freddy Nelson. Fluffy blonde hair dishevelled, he's grabbing onto the bar like he's hanging off the edge of a cliff. Skinny jeans so low they are almost below his thighs, his eyes wild, his mouth opening every few seconds to shout words like "WOWSER"—"REVVING"— and "GOD YEAH!" in a high-pitched yelp—before clothes-lining all the drinks off the bar with both arms.

I walk over to the bar for a closer look and the girl follows. Bran and Jackson are in fits of laughter. Inez is trying to give Nelson some water. "Freddy... Freddy," she says in her high-pitched Spanish accent.

He half stumbles—grabs a random drink and pours it down his front.

"Don't worry," I say to the girl. "He works here too."

*

I get one or two nights off a week—if I'm lucky. Jeremy manages in my place. Well, he does his best. I still get twenty-five phone calls a night when things go wrong— tonight, he calls saying someone has just been glassed on the dance floor. What should he do? I say an ambulance might be a good idea. Looking back on it, I should have chosen someone more reliable like Freddy Maytal or Cub to be assistant manager. But Jeremy has been here longer than they have and maybe it wouldn't make any difference anyway. The interference of man is futile. Places like this are built to go wrong.

*

Meet Tattoo Paul, the cleanest man in here. He has not drunk or taken drugs for twenty years. The cloakroom is his domain. His vices are tattoos, roll-ups, and tea.

Like the merciful manager I am, I cover him for a ciga-rette break again, staring into the face of a moody girl with a nose ring who wants to know why she can't put her coat in for free. Her eyes are glazed. The DJ is playing 'Road to Nowhere' by Talking Heads.

"Paul lets me."

"I'm not Paul."

"Where is he?"

"Heaven."

"You're a prick."

She fiddles with her purse.

"Look, come on, it's only a pound. Is it really going to ruin your night if you have to pay?"

I think she's about to relent, but she looks me in the eyes and says—"Why do you think you're better than everyone else? Just because you're posh, I do not fear you."

She leaves with her coat on, bunched up around her neck and shoulders like Cruella de Vil. A few seconds later, Paul comes back.

"Alright, mate."

"You're too kind to these cretins," I say.

"It's Paul's Coat Room Emporium."

"Some girl just called me posh…"

"Ah, tally ho, Bertie, did they call you posh? Fancy that, darling."

We talk posh for a while and I sit with him for a bit, swigging Coke from the can and eating the box of Roses that he invariably has in here—he only gives them out to pretty girls. They might even get a few if they have a tattoo.

*

An hour before closing time, I watch Cruella girl with the nose ring crawl to the bar and beg for water.

*

Thursday's Indie night. It's called Empire and run by a little chap called Kyle who is covered in tattoos, wears jeans with a chain, and has three piercings in each ear—a spirited sort of guy who it's impossible not to like. He's good for playing anything you want, and early on in the evening, I'm feeling a bit morose so go to him with a large large large vodka and ask him to play three Smiths' songs in a row, starting with 'This Charming Man', 'How Soon is Now' in between, and finishing with 'Pretty Girls Make Graves'.

*

Meet Harrison. He's worked here as long as I have and is a bassist in a band on the brink of the big time—they've played here twice and have their name on the wall. He wears skinny jeans, derby shoes, a denim jacket, and a burgundy-coloured beanie hat. He also has a beard that makes it look like he lives in the wild when he's not here, which is more and more now his band is getting popular.

I'm walking past the toilets to my office at the end of Empire night when I hear him shout from the Gents'.

"What?"

He emerges holding a tower of plastic cups making a sound which is halfway between laughter and utter disgust, and with a screwed-up face.

"Have a look in there."

The Gents' walls are covered in shit—thick brown stains drip down the mirrors from stinking blobs of crap.

"What the fuck?"

Mike is at my shoulder.

All we can do is stare and wonder what sort of person paints the walls with excrement.

*

At the end of the night, Mike and I troll through the CCTV cameras for answers.

We watch a group of guys all wearing blue and yellow t-shirts that say LACROSSE SOCIETY come into the Gents'. Our viewpoint is from just above the entrance, looking at the cubicles. One of them is holding a pint and he goes into the right-hand cubicle and takes a piss without shutting the door. Another guy goes into the left-hand cubicle and does shut the door. The others go off camera to the urinals. After about ten seconds, the first guy finishes his piss and comes out to the sinks, stands in front of the mirror and downs his pint. Then he fills it up with water and goes over to the engaged cubicle and throws the water over the door. He turns and laughs. Soon, the other two get involved throwing water over the door. Then something dark comes flying over from within the cubicle and splats on the mirror. The door opens and the guy who has been doused in water has something in his hands raised to throw, a wild grin on his face. He throws it before disappearing back into his cubicle for more ammunition. Meanwhile, one of his mates runs into the other cubicle, takes down his jeans and sits down without shutting the door. After about ten seconds, he stands up, rolls out some toilet paper, and dips his hands into the pan.

"Dirty fuckers!" says Mike.

In this manner, the situation unfolds, until they all wash their hands and exit.

*

Years mean nothing to me. It doesn't matter what month it is. Weeks pass like days. Hours no longer exist. They go far too quickly, sitting at home, alone, smoking and thinking about the people I used to know, too numb to think, too cold to feel, and before I know it, the day's over, like someone hidden in my wall has been pressing fast forward on my life. No wonder I don't get anything done on my days off. And then, when I'm back in that wretched building, walking around in the day when nobody else is around, shoes sticking to the floor, the place reeking of sweat left to fester, puke cleaned up but still lingering, the clinical whiff of every evil alcohol—time crawls. Maintenance. The beer order. Paperwork. Step outside for a smoke. Watch the cars go by. Back inside, to the jobs I don't have to think about but which have to be done.

Unlike Terry, Karen and Dom, my office is downstairs, deep in the basement, next to the cloakroom and the toilets and the fire escape. No windows to the outside world, no connection to anything. I could sit through a hurricane, through the rapture, holed up against nothing, staring at the pin board, the computer from 1998, the keyboard covered in fag ash. There's no phone signal down here. I'm unreachable. It is my domain.

Take my phone out of my pocket. Look at the screen. See a text a few hours old from a number I deleted weeks ago. At least, I deleted it from my address book weeks ago. If only I could delete it from my mind as easily.

I'll be coming round tomorrow to pick the rest of my stuff up. Please make sure you are not there. I'll put the key back through the letterbox. C

*

We're sitting downstairs after hours with a crate of beer and cigarettes spread over the round tables. The bouncers are grouped by the door, drinking their usual one before bedtime, swearing and re-enacting fights. I haven't cashed up yet and I'm already on my third beer and second large vodka. There are a few faces I don't recognise but that isn't unusual. Munks' after-hours lock-ins are infamous. I'm used to walking back out into the club to find a bunch of random people drinking my beer. Although, with the new owners, who knows how long this will be allowed to continue?

We're talking about Jackson's sexuality.

"So, are you gay too?" asks a girl I don't know.

"One third," says Jackson.

"One-third gay?"

He nods.

"Postman," says Bran. He is restless—glancing over at the bouncers. I've told him he's allowed to smoke a joint when they leave.

"That's right," says Jackson. "Postman, not a post box."

"Unlike Jeremy here," I say.

Jeremy is the laziest gay I've ever met. He hasn't cut his hair for years. Cub says his room is a hole and I don't doubt it.

"Nah… I drink too much to have a boyfriend," he says in his odd, squeaky voice.

We finish the crate before I stumble to the office, leaving them to open another whilst I sit there, staring at the screen but not seeing it, trying to remember how to count, tired beyond tired, clinging to the end of a long day, the longest in the last line, but all my thoughts just keep coming back round to the one that hurts—the reason why I don't want to go home.

*

Next door is a sanctuary. It is called The Bellhop—owned by the same guy who used to own Munks, who now leases the building to Terry and Karen's company. He owns most of Gin Lane, the aptly named street where most of the city's bars and clubs are located. A lot of people think Munks and The Bellhop are the same place. It's an easy mistake to make—both of them are grimy cellar bars full of the same people, with an aimless, comfortable existence that ends at closing time and begins when the doors open the next morning. Although, in The Bellhop, we wear our day faces. I spend too much time there. It's all too easy to.

If you think about it, it isn't really a sanctuary at all.

*

Dubstep night. The night from hell. Pale faces in a dead zone. We make no money on the bar, but serve lots of water and energy drink for the robots with jaws stuck in motion, chewing until 4 am when we kick them out. Then we find dozens of empty drug bags abandoned on the floor and think—thank God it's all over for another month.

Apart from Bran. For some reason, he loves dubstep and listens to it every morning.

*

Friday night, and I'm in the office counting money ready to pay a band called The Vaccines that have just played and who pulled in quite a big crowd, when Cub bangs on the door in a panic. It's just after midnight and Freddy Nelson is fucked out of his head and Karen is still around, looking for any reason to sack someone. Usually, she and Terry aren't seen dead in this place after 9 o'clock. They leave all the hard nighttime labour to me.

"Hide him in the cloakroom," I suggest.

*

Freddy Nelson is conked out on the floor of the cloakroom with a wooden spoon shoved down his pants.

Mike, Tattoo Paul, Bran, and I stand at the entrance,

watching him snore. Someone has written the words **I TOUCH KIDS** on his face in black pen.

"How did this happen?" I ask.

Bran starts laughing, "Nelson."

Tattoo Paul says, "Revving."

Freddy Nelson looks up with one eye open and a crooked smile—"God yeah!"

*

Outside, early evening, leaning on the railings and looking at the road below, half listening to a chatty guy who is currently our only customer, wishing night would fall, wishing I hadn't drunk so much last night.

"So, what do you do, man?" asks my fledgling companion.

"I'm the manager."

"And what about when you're not the manager?"

"I sleep."

"Don't you do anything else? Play music?"

"I used to take pictures."

"Why did you stop?"

"My camera broke."

I pitch my fag down onto the road below and go back inside, past Bran behind the upstairs bar, who is getting paid to just sit on Facebook, and down the stairs to barricade myself in my office until later.

*

I wake up one morning to five missed calls and four texts, all from the same person.

Are you awake yet? What's happening with you and C? X
Call me when you wake up. Or skype, as it is free? X
Are you still remembering to take your medication?? xx
Please get in touch. I'm worried. Mum. Xx

*

Monday night—we just open the café and the upstairs bar for a night called Acoustic Array run by a nice kid called Jason whose parents are friends with Terry. He makes no money himself but likes putting on local artists. He appears permanently stoned even though he doesn't smoke.

The club downstairs is dark and empty. I'm on the bar with Karen, who's useless and ends up offending everyone. She's worse on the pumps than Shelly and worse with people than Pete Bone.

I finish an hour before closing, she wants to cash up on her own even though it takes her hours and she messed it up when she first tried to do it last week. Just before I leave to go for a pint in the pub next door, I'm rolling a cigarette by the bar hatch and listening to a guy playing acoustic guitar, when I hear Karen arguing with a girl who has just paid for a cider and blackcurrant and is examining her change. She's been overcharged. I walk away, smiling, as a middle-aged man begins arguing in defence of the girl.

*

The owners have called a staff meeting. All the bar staff are here, but only a few of the bouncers. Karen does most of the talking. I hang around at the back of the pack, knowing what's coming next.

"What is happening with the staff contracts?" asks Cub.

"We're still working on them," says Karen.

"Still?" says Jackson.

Karen glares at him, "You will understand how important it is to get things right first time."

I'm impressed that nobody laughs in the inevitable silence.

"And, erm… as I am sure some of you are already aware, we're going to be looking out for some new staff."

"Why?" asks Jackson.

Karen looks at me.

"Because we bought a business here that we want to expand. We like to think of Munks as a family, and we want to extend that family. We want some new blood." She gives a forced smile. "So, if any of you have any friends who you think might want to work here, give me their details. Terry and I will start interviewing next week."

Nobody says anything.

"Also," says Karen, "you may have seen the signs we have put up around the venue…"

I look at one of their signs, up on the wall behind the upstairs bar—**MUNKS: THE FUTURE!**

"And we just want to reiterate how important it is to not call this place a nightclub. That may have been the direction the previous owner chose, but not us. Munks is a live music venue. You only have to look at the names we've put on the walls to see that. And to spread this idea, we need it to begin with you guys. If we hear anybody calling it a nightclub, we will correct you."

Jackson is bursting to say something. He has a pained look on his face and he keeps biting his nails.

Inez speaks up—"Will our hours be changing?"

"Sorry, Inez?"

"Our hours—will there be any change to them, Karen?"

Karen nods. "I know that you have grown used to your fixed hours under the previous regime and in the transition period, but do not be surprised if they begin to be cut down slightly whilst we head into the quieter period of business…"

Nobody says anything but everyone wants to.

Karen, who has just become the Devil, says, "Now, I think Dom has a few things to add…"

"Erm… yeah, so… we're going to be launching a new night soon…" says Dom. And he whines on, legs crossed, hands flapping. He has to be gay.

*

Meet the lost girls. Their makeup smudged, their clothes dishevelled, their eyes wet with drink. You will find them under the flashing lights of the dance floor at the end of a Cheese Night, singing along to 'Holding out for a Hero' without truly realising the meaning of the words.

*

I'm sitting with Cub, Bran, Jackson and Harrison, another Cheese over and done with.

They're asking me about the new staff interviews.

I roll a cigarette and pop off the cap of a fresh bottle of Coors with Bran's lighter.

"I have no power here anymore, guys," I say.

Cub is wearing an extra-large t-shirt with a picture of a laughing skull on it. It swathes her thin frame.

"They're going to fuck this place up," she says. "Is it true they want to open a record shop?"

Bran starts laughing. He has his headphones in. He does this everywhere—sitting here with us, walking down the street, behind the bar when it's quiet, next door when we're drinking and watching the football—he'll bop away to his dubstep, in a world of his own.

Then Jackson starts laughing—a loud, strangled, staccato howl like a dog.

Soon we're all laughing.

*

Karen is complaining to me about the staff being on Facebook when they're supposed to be working.

"Blame Mark Zuckerberg," I tell her, and to her credit, she gives me a half smile.

It was either that or blame her for putting a computer in the upstairs bar.

*

Another Thursday night and Harrison comes to me again and says, "There are people shagging in the Gents'."

Mike is with me in the office and the three of us go to the Gents' and stand looking at the left-hand cubicle. The door is shaking, and from within come the unmistakable noises of a nightclub sexual encounter.

We look underneath the door and see a pair of white trainers with dropped jeans and an open belt around the ankles, and girls' clothes all over the floor which is grimy and wet and utterly disgusting.

I knock on the door—"Hello!"

Mike knocks—"Stop fucking shagging, you dirty fuckers."

Harrison and I start cracking up.

I knock again—"Cease intercourse!"

The door rattles in a steady rhythm.

Mike grabs hold of the top of the door, lifts himself up and pops his head over to take a look.

He drops down and says, "She's fucking naked… not wearing a stitch."

I knock again and then lever myself up to look down on something which you could try with all your might to forget but never will.

They both have their backs turned to the cubicle door—he stands behind her and she is leaning over the toilet with her arms planted on either side of the cistern, looking down into the depths of the pan. On the stained light green wall above them, someone has scrawled the words **FUCK FOREVER** in black pen. She turns her head and I see one half-open eye—smiling in a drunken stupor.

We have to wait until they're finished—spend five minutes knocking and shouting, and only getting yelps in reply. Finally, he gives one final, conclusive, drawn-out cry. Then silence.

Mike bangs on the door again—"Get the fuck out!"

We hear them scrabbling around.

The door opens three and a half minutes later and they emerge. She has her top on backwards, there are stains down her skirt and her hair is all over the place. They both have shameless smiles on.

*

Meet Madsen. He looks like Robert Downey Jnr would if he'd done more drugs in the 80s and 90s. He also has a knighthood, according to his driving license. Back in the dark days when I was just a humble bartender, he used to DJ here as a member of the Slugs—a three-piece DJ outfit (Desmond, the lead singer of Harrison's band, was also one of them). They turned the upstairs bar into a funk house emporium, a drug parlour, and a pit of hedonism. Madsen has a knack for offending people and he fell out with the previous owner, Ian, for one reason or another—probably some drug-related fuck-up. He's old school for a DJ these days and brings his own vinyl—an eclectic mix of reggae, Motown and jazz. Dom has finally done something right and got him back to play at weekends.

"So, when do you want me to start, boss?" he says with a wink, walking in with an old green satchel bag full of vinyl that he must have had when he was at school. He wears the jeans and trainers of a younger man and speaks with the chilled-out drawl of someone who is constantly stoned.

"You know how it is, Matt—set up, have a pint, a few fags, then play when it gets busy."

"Cool."

He tries to pay Laura for his Grolsch but I tell her to write it down on the wastage sheet.

"How many is he allowed?" she asks. Madsen has his headphones on at the DJ booth, looks over and gives me a thumbs up.

'The Israelites' by Desmond Derrick comes on through the big speakers.

"As many as he can drink. Just don't tell anyone. Oh, and don't give him any shots."

*

Cleaning the lines late on a Wednesday when we're closed and have been all night because the town is dead. This is the only purification this place gets. An hour a week after I've done the ordering, I pump water through the old pipes, put pipe cleaner through, flush them out with water and reattach the barrels. I'm left with a pint and a half from each tap, lined up on the bar. I go upstairs and send Bran and Harrison a text—

Line cleaning. Get down here. Pints to drink.

*

Meet Freddy Maytal—the nicest guy in the world. He graduated with a music degree last year but is still here, no fixed abode, sofa surfing—currently on Cub and Jeremy's. Along with the rest of his band, he's been about to move to Brighton for a year now. I don't want to lose him—these days, an experienced bar hand isn't as easy to find as you'd think. He's also handy to have around when musical stuff goes wrong. I can push a few buttons and dials but I'm no technician. The wires in this place have been hooked up since the 70s and no one, not even Jeff, truly understands the mechanics. Freddy Maytal is perhaps the only guy who has half an idea because Jeff is losing his marbles and starting to get preoccupied with sex like only a Northern man in his fifties can. Just the other day, I'd finished reading a Venue magazine with Kylie Minogue on the front, when he came up to the bar for a pint after sound-checking the last band, saw the magazine and said, "Oooh, Kylie—do you mind if I take her home for later?"

*

There are four bouncers on the books—Mike, Bill, Sam, and Pete Bone—but the rest of them and all the DJs get paid cash in hand on the night. Ten past four and the staff are cleaning up. I walk through the club with five bags of cash and a receipt for each to sign. Upstairs, Madsen is pissed and mumbling. He asks if he can leave his records in the cloakroom until next week. I leave him to sign the bit of paper with his name on it whilst I go to deal with a commotion by the door. When I come back, he hands it over and I start chuckling. It looks like a kid has drawn all over it—all I can make out is a swastika and then the words **KAREN AND TERRY GO FUCK YOURSELFS.**

*

Thursday again. It's cold and I'm shivering outside, watching them all queue to get in, the guys dressed in t-shirts, the girls in skirts, their breath mingling in a permanent white haze above them. Arctic Monkeys 'I Bet You Look Good On The Dancefloor' is playing inside. Mike is at my side, gloves on, breathing into them, shiny head glistening.

"Guy about halfway up. Pink Ralph Lauren t-shirt. Blue jeans. Trainers. Short dark hair. Recognise him?"

I look at the guy for a few seconds, dip my head to relight my fag which keeps going out, and nod.

Mike smiles.

We wait until he's at the front of the queue, some twenty minutes later, and Mike points a finger at the chap and says, "You! You're not coming in—you're banned for life."

People's ears prick up when they hear *banned for life.*

At first, he's stunned—"What?" Then he starts arguing. "Why? What have I done?"

"For throwing shit around the Gents' toilets last month."

His face goes white. Then bright red. There are a few sniggers, then the girls who'd previously been huddling up to him are standoffish, unobtainable.

As the queue moves forward, he is lost.

*

All the staff are gone. I'm alone in the office at 6 in the morning with a beer and a plastic cup full of fag butts, playing music from my iPod through a battered set of Bose speakers. The song playing is 'Short Change Hero' by the Heavy. I go to the cellar for more beer. Walking through the dark, I can't see anything but I don't need to. I know where everything is. There is no such thing as fear here—it is too close to daybreak.

Fumbling around in the beer crate. Wind on my face. Puffing on my cigarette but it's gone out. This is when the fear comes. I hear a noise from the next room where there's a door that leads to the old tunnels—the ones that run beneath the city—blocked off somewhere down the line by the dirt, the decay, the husks of broken furniture, the rubbish and bottles that have come through the iron bars from the pavement above.

The door rattles on its hinges. It is locked and I have the keys.

But am I the only one?

*

Please don't ignore me, son. I'm sorry about everything. I'm worried about you. We both are. Remember that. I'm going to stop pestering you now. Here when you are ready to talk. We love you. Mum and Frank x

*

Fading into the drunken darkness at the end of another long night, left all alone in the club, hearing songs from another life, immune to all drink and smoking one cigarette after another. Looking at my watch I see it's past 6 am, so I open a drawer, take my pills out and swallow them with warm Coors Light. Then I finish cashing up, put the final numbers into the spreadsheet, and open up Internet Explorer to look at the most recent searches in the Google taskbar:

lindsay lohan no arm
my mum moved away
does a rotten egg sink or float

*

Dom has launched his new Friday night. Not that he needed to because it's a Friday night and it's always busy. He's called it Desire, of which I have absolutely none. Madsen plays reggae upstairs and Dom has roped in a guy called Aaron, an emo who never grew out of it and who is covered in piercings and tattoos. He has to get the train in from the next city to play electro/pop/indie/house for five hours in return for £150 and a crate of beer rider to himself.

Two things you must learn about DJs—they often leave pints of piss in the booth because they are too lazy to go to the toilet, and they get paid too much to care.

*

Meet the wild bunch, still clamouring for booze at half-past three on the last Friday of the month—going nuts, tipping all manner of liquor down their throats. The bars are packed, we've run out of vodka and Tequila because Terry cocked up the order and they keep wanting more and more drink, anything to slake a thirst that knows no bounds, there's been three fights, two puddles of vomit and a blocked toilet and I can't remember the last time I slept, I get the bouncers to clear everyone out of the upstairs bar and shut it early, take the till downstairs to the office with Mike at my shoulder in case anyone decides to get smart and greedy—into the office, lock the door, light a cigarette, and wait for it all to be over.

*

A quiet Monday and I'm in doing paperwork for a few hours. The acoustic night was called off but Karen insisted we open anyway—for 'drinkers'. Terry has returned the

responsibility of ordering stock to me after his last cata-
strophic fuck-up. Upstairs, Karen's first new employee is
on his trial shift—a smiling black guy called Thomas who
is being shown the ropes by Freddy Maytal.

At ten o'clock I go up—the place is empty.

"Any customers?"

Freddy shakes his head.

"Have we taken any money at all?"

"Nope."

"Well, at least Karen picked a great night for your trial
shift," I say to Thomas, who just smiles awkwardly.

When he goes, and it's just Freddy and me, sitting with
a bottle of beer and a fag, I ask him how Thomas got on.

He shakes his head. "It was a good job we had no customers."

I laugh—"Karen knows how to pick them."

*

You can usually find me here towards the end of the night,
in the last half hour when I've taken the door till and we
stop letting in. I stand with Mike on the edge of it all,
leaning against the wall and watching the chaos come to
an end. Chaos caused by the most destructive drug in the
world.

Tonight, I'm particularly interested in the middle-aged
man in a suit who has been standing at the bar all night,
drinking Famous Grouse on the rocks, one after another,
and staring out onto the dance floor at the woman he

came in with—his wife. I saw their wedding rings when they paid at the door till and I stamped their hands. His wife is a tall, blonde woman with a taut face that has a cocaine sheen. Her drink, a gin and tonic he ordered with his first whiskey, has remained on the bar all night—the ice now melted, condensation creeping across the glass. As the night went on, his posture slowly slipped into a drunken prop, his hair somehow more wild and askew, his shirt untucked. Now, his eyes point crookedly out into the dead zone with an ill glaze that puts fear in my heart.

I point him out to Mike who nods, then shakes his head with a small grimace that means he sees trouble coming. Then we both look out onto the dance floor for the man's wife, and see her by the wall, dancing with another man—gyrating to Missy Elliot's 'Lose Control' up against a young chap who can't believe his luck. He has a hand up the back of her short skirt. She nuzzles his neck like she's biting him, moving faster against him. Surely it's only a matter of time before this goes way too far.

Mike puts a hand on my shoulder—we shrug at each other, then he goes through the door that leads to the small kitchen, the downstairs bar, and the cellar, and flicks one of the light switches on the panel by the bar entrance to tell the DJ this is the last song. Then he makes a stupid face at Cub, sticks his tongue out and starts humping Bran from behind who is standing on the pump closest to the kitchen serving a couple of pints of cider. I laugh. Try to forget about the man and his wife. Try and shake off the horrible feeling that something bad is going to happen, somewhere, to somebody, tonight, when we close the doors behind them and shut them out into the night.

A few minutes later, the lights are on and people are blinking. The middle-aged man at the bar is gone, his wife's drink untouched and an empty plastic tumbler the only signs that he was ever there. His wife is leading the young guy by the hand, up the steps from the dance floor. I watch them disappear upstairs and out of here, as Sam and Pete Bone start shouting for everyone to clear off, and the mob look around delirious, while we get to work cleaning up after them.

I start to pick up the hundreds of bottles and plastic cups that litter the place. And those are just the empties. There are countless full, half-full, and quarter-full drinks around the place—paid for, sipped and abandoned. I get a slop bucket and empty them all in.

How much booze do we throw away at the end of the night?

Too much.

*

Mike, Pete Bone, Shelly, and I are watching a grown man on the CCTV screen take a shit in the corner of the club.

"The dirty cunt is actually doing it!" says Pete Bone, and he and Mike rush downstairs.

Shelly and I watch them stand next to him, wait until he pulls his trousers up with a silly grin on his face, and just as he's reaching for something—maybe toilet roll—they grab him by the arms and haul him out of the picture.

On the control panel beside the screen, the light next to **DOWNSTAIRS FIREDOOR** comes on and starts beeping.

*

The doormen aren't happy. Mike comes to me after we shut on Thursday and tells me that Karen has told him they only want three bouncers on a Saturday from now on.

"On a Saturday? Is she fucking mental? It's the busiest night of the fucking week."

I nod. "She asked me to do the same with the bar staff."

"You're joking."

"Nope—she seemed to think we could cope with one upstairs and two down."

"What did you say?"

"I told her that's fine as long as she and Terry are prepared to come in and work the bar too."

He laughs. "Stupid bitch. What the fuck are they doing?"

"Slashing their outgoings, mate. Big time."

"And they've just spent how much on a fucking brand-new bar, café, fucking kitchen coming soon, record shop or whatever bollocks. Fucking hell. I think I preferred it when Ian owned it."

I smile. "You're not the first to say that. And you won't be the last."

When he leaves, I minimise the cash sheet document and open up Internet Explorer. I shake my head, bewildered, as I read over the latest Google searches.

lie in or lye in
where to buy faith shoes
should i leave my boyfriend if he won't marry me

*

It's not always Freddy Nelson who is paralytic here on his night off. Sometimes it's Jeremy slurring and stumbling around, and often Bran, who can be a real shit when he drinks vodka and Red Bull—I must tell all the staff not to serve it to him because he starts fighting everyone. Even Freddy Maytal has been known to have a real blowout from time to time, where he becomes even more excitable—it usually ends with him tiring himself out and falling asleep on a girl's leg.

And the manager?

On his night off, he won't be seen within a hundred yards of this place.

Except for in the pub next door.

*

Karen comes to me and tells me that she and Terry don't want Jeremy doing the assistant managing anymore.

"Why?" I ask.

"He's got too slack. As have a lot of the old staff. They have bad attitudes."

I think we have different opinions on what constitutes a bad attitude.

"OK—well, who do you want me to replace him with?"

She purses her lips—"Can you train up Dom?"

My laughter is surely all the answer she needs, but as she's still standing in front of me, I say—"Don't you need someone who is able to stay up past midnight?"

"You forget that Dom works all day."

"So do I."

"We don't ask you to."

"Who else is going to do this?" and I gesture at my computer screen where I'm doing the final wage sheet ready to email to their accountant.

She bites her lip. Looks at my desk—coffee cups with mould and fungus growing inside them (my science project), fag butts, bottles of beer, scraps of paper with strange phallic biro drawings on them (Mike), an origami swan I made one night when I wanted to shut out the noise and the dickheads from Dub Step night.

Her eyes move to the wall where I have all manner of things stuck to the large cork board—a wage packet for Abasi from months ago that I keep forgetting to give him, a ticket to Glastonbury 2007, a picture of Kurt Cobain, a list headed **WHOSE TURN IS IT TO CLEAN UP THE PUKE**, an old bank card belonging to a HUGH JANUS that I found a few years ago, a phone number with **JONES, ELECTRICIAN** written underneath in my handwriting, though I can't recall putting it there.

She leaves before the issue can be resolved. Later, I get an email from her telling me to tidy up my office.

*

6 am on a Sunday—a lock-in for the desperate, the drunk, the damaged, the disturbed.

Bran and Inez are conversing in her mother tongue. For all of his misadventure, Bran can speak pretty good Spanish, but only when he's really pissed. I'm drinking through a hangover, while Jackson is sitting in silence with hollow eyes watching Madsen who is listening to 'She's Lost Control' by Joy Division over and over again on Jackson's iPod, singing in a monotone drawl—"I want to do drugs again. I want to do drugs again. I want to do drugs again."

The place is a charnel house. I've just realised that there are still cups and bottles and paper towels and other crap everywhere.

"Guys," I say, "have you cleaned up?"

It takes several minutes to get a response but by that time we're all singing along to Madsen's version of Joy Division and I couldn't care less about the state of the dance floor.

*

Less than five hours later, I haven't slept and I'm drinking Bloody Marys at the bar in The Bellhop. Soon, Karen and

Terry want to open the café in the day and then, surely, I will have no existence outside the job I don't get paid enough for.

The only thing that makes me feel better is to run in here for a quick drink whenever I get a chance. The bar staff are all friends of mine, so they give me and my staff cheap drinks and get the same treatment when they come to Munks. It is an unofficial yet steadfast agreement and one that cannot be spoken of under any circumstances.

On the wall behind the bar is a newspaper clipping that reads **DO YOU LIKE BEING THE CENTRE OF ATTENTION?**

*

I exist on windows of sleep and a rigorous timetable of booze and cigarettes. I eat on occasions and strictly abstain from all drugs except those prescribed to me by my doctor.

*

Meet Bret. He wears a trilby hat and has a scruffy beard. He is a student, a writer, an experienced bar hand. Karen has just hired him. His first shift has just ended and he's sitting with us after hours like he belongs here.

Bran asks me if he can use my card to buy some new trainers online.

"Of course, mate."

I have to explain to Bret that Bran doesn't have his own bank account.

"He has also been barred from this place twice," says Harrison, "haven't you, AC?"

He shrugs, "I just keep coming back."

"What did you do?" asks Bret.

"It's our manager's fault," he says.

"What? How?"

"It was your birthday. We were both in on the piss."

"Oh yeah, so it was."

"And AC here is standing at the bar," says Harrison, "and he snorts some coke out of his hand, and the manager at the time, John, I think it was, sees him, sacks him, and bars him on the spot. Our manager here got him his job back when the new owners took over."

"Bran will still be working here when we are all dead," I say.

"Why do you call him AC?" Bret asks Harrison.

Harrison shrugs, "No idea."

*

One of my predecessors is getting married. He's the one who taught me all the locks, how to decipher the cash sheet, and jangle keys. Unfortunately, with no ass man and crap bosses, I can't get the night off.

But I don't mind. There are lots of people going who I don't want to see.

*

Meet Dave Abbott. One of the few external promoters who still runs a night in this place. The originator of Cheese Night, House DJ extraordinaire, a family man who chain smokes Marlboros and has a nervous twitch in one eye. Friends with Annie Mac and other big DJ names who I can never remember. He also runs a few guest nights once a month, big house music DJ nights that pull the punters in—RAM and BROOKLYN.

We're in the office and I'm giving him his split after another busy Cheese.

"There you go, mate," and I print off the receipt and give him what he's due in cash. He gets a 50/50 door split after I've paid Clive the DJ (who has done this night since time began) and the doormen.

"Cheers, mate, I can pay for the car's service now."

He scribbles a signature and pockets his cash.

"There's always something else to pay for," I say.

He agrees and I follow him up and out of the club.

After he's gone, I stand outside considering the short walk to the side of the building to close the fire exits, listening to the drunken conversations that you need to be pissed to understand, when I hear a grating, rattling sound, followed by a bang and I look down to see Dave Abbott driving past in his Clio. He gives me a wave, fag on the go, window open. I send him a text telling him to get his car looked at first thing in the morning.

*

I sit down, all cashed up, done for the night, fucked.

They are all drunk. Bret and Jackson are discussing Shakespeare. Bran and Harrison are talking football. Jeremy is rambling to himself, cross-eyed, drinking directly from the bottle of staff vodka.

The conversations reach a natural pause—people are rolling cigarettes.

Only Jeremy continues jabbering—like he's performing all the parts in a bad play.

I finish preparing my cigarette, look up and say:

"Jeremy, is there any point to what you're saying?"

*

Meet Dancing Man. He wears chunky white trainers, black jeans with a belt, and a white crew-neck t-shirt tucked in. It is 10:30 on a Tuesday and I have just opened the doors. Harrison comes to find me in the office to announce that Dancing Man is here. I follow him out into the club. Dancing Man is at the bar chatting shit to Cub who has just served him his usual two double vodka and lemonades—because "they're cheap." He picks them up, crosses the empty dance floor, puts his drinks on the shelf at the edge, and steps up onto the stage.

"Wait for it," says Harrison, nudging me, as Dancing Man approaches the DJ booth.

When Backstreet Boys ends, 'Disco Inferno' comes on.

"Here he goes…"

Dancing Man goes wild, jumps off the stage onto the dance floor and starts pumping his arms, hopping around with a big goofy grin on his face.

"Burn, baby, burn," I say.

We watch him dance for three songs, until more people arrive, which is when Dancing Man grabs his drinks and vacates the dance floor, his routine over until next time.

*

Meet Jordan Bone, aka DJ Euro Pigeon, three times DMC champion, and resident DJ of Munks. He ties his long black hair up in a hairband, it's been this length since I've known him. He wears a baggy white t-shirt, baggy jeans, and usually a moustache that looks out of place because of his tanned skin. He's persuaded Terry and Dom to run a hip hop night on the night that nobody can solve (Wednesday) and he gets a good crowd in. His mates, the breakdancers, come down and make surreal shapes on the dance floor, and people are clapping and standing in a circle, and I stand at the steps by the toilets, looking down at the contortionists and wishing that all nights could be like this.

*

I got this job through a friend. That's how everyone gets the job here. Most of them are students who need to earn their beer money because their loan won't cover it and the bank won't extend their overdraft. I was just one of the crowd. Only, while everyone else moved on after graduating with their useless degree and a big debt, I stayed because I didn't have any other plans. I get messages from them sometimes, these people I once knew, who now exist in another walk of life, who might as well be strangers, and who all ask me what I'm doing and whether I'm still at Munks, usually because they are coming back here for the weekend and want to get in for free.

I don't tend to reply to them.

*

Karen has hired more staff. Georgie, a stocky drama student with piercings and bleached shoulder-length hair, and Daniel, another drama student, who looks uncannily like Jackson, only more innocent—the pretty boy version.

On her first shift, someone comes to the bar and asks Georgie for a Jägerbomb. I'm standing by the till doing nothing and she says, "Erm… yeah…" and looks at me for help.

"I thought you were a student?" I say to her as I show her how to pour the drink that she will soon be able to do in her sleep.

Daniel is a little more confident behind the bar, although in the lock-in after hours, he says that Karen has hired him to run the 'Record Shop' when it opens. He chats a lot of other shit as well but this one I can't blame him for.

*

"Did you know that she's sleeping upstairs on a camp bed?" I say to Mike, Bill and Stacie on the door.

"You're joking," says Stacie.

I shake my head.

It's early on a Friday night and we're talking about Karen, while in the next room, Madsen is playing 'Uptown Top Ranking' by Althea and Donna.

"Crazy bint," Pete Bone chips in from the entrance where he's stamping customers as they come in.

"Did I hear that she has a flat in London?" asks Stacie.

"Yep," I say, "although she doesn't go back very often."

"No husband then?" says Mike.

"You've got to be joking," says Pete Bone. "Who would want to sleep with that?"

"Wasn't she staying upstairs in The Bellhop for a while?" asks Mike.

"Yeah," I say, "for a while. Then Ian told her to get out."

"I'm not surprised," says Pete Bone.

"Do you know who she reminds me of?" I say.

"Who?"

"Dorothy."

"Oh fuck!"

Mike is nodding. "Yeah."

Bill—"Definitely."

Dorothy is one of my predecessors. Ian, the old owner of Munks and current owner of The Bellhop, is her brother. Down the years, he has barred her from both of his establishments a number of times.

"She was fucking bonkers," says Mike.

"Screw loose," says Stacie.

"Pete, do you remember when she asked you and me to use, how did she put it?—*dignified restraint* when throwing people out?"

Pete scoffs, "Dignified restraint… what a load of fucking bollocks."

"Me and Karina bumped into her in Sainsbury's the other day," says Mike. "Dappy mare roped my missus into meeting her for coffee. I said to her later—rather you than me." He laughs. "And if that wasn't enough, just as we're trying to get away from her, she pulls out this shoebox and shows us these heels she's just bought. Bright red they were. About five inches on the bloody things, and starts yapping about this chap who is about 35 or something who she's fucking."

"35?" says Stacie, "but she must be almost 60."

"Yeah," says Mike. "Anyway, she says to me, jokingly, and fortunately my missus is alright with stuff like this from working here and because she knows Dorothy—but she asks me if she should wear them later when meeting up with this young guy."

"The teenager?" I ask.

"Yeah, may as well be, the dirty old minx. But she says to me, *what would you do if you saw me in these?* And, well, you know her, you have to play up to her because she is so fucking mad, so I said—*probably drag you into the bedroom.*"

We cringe in unison.

Pete Bone says, "You dirty fucking tease."

Mike wipes the sweat off his forehead and says, "I was thinking—*run a fucking mile.*"

"Fuck off," says Pete Bone, who is looking at the window.

"What?"

"Look who it is."

We look up and see Dorothy, dressed in her glad rags, crazy grey hair all over the place. Waving. Smiling. Poking her head around the door. Patting Sam on the shoulder and cackling.

"Hi boys!"

Blowing kisses. Rubbing Sam's arm harder and making him look very uncomfortable.

"Is she wearing the red shoes?" I say.

"I don't want to know," says Stacie.

"Not talking about me, are you?" she shrieks through the door.

We smile and say of course not, a row of guilty faces at a shooting gallery.

*

Meet the middle-aged man making a scene by the front door because he's been refused entry for being too drunk.

He remonstrates with Sam and Stacie in his corduroy blazer, chinos, and light purple cravat, using long words that I'm sure Sam doesn't know the meanings of. Stacie is ignoring him and chatting up the girls who are smoking and watching with interest.

Finally, the remonstrator asks to see the manager.

Sam turns to look at me, the usual blank and bored expression on his face, the white fleck of chewing gum occasionally visible as his jaw goes up and down. I'm standing half-hidden in shadow, leaning against the wall and smoking. The man turns to me, crosses his arms and begins his case from the beginning.

I sigh. After so many years in this job, you'd think I would have learnt how to disappear entirely.

*

On the upstairs bar, there is a place we call Shot's Corner, a four-yard space that is out of camera. It doesn't officially exist and should never be spoken of, at least not too loudly. Sometimes, when it is really dead, you will find me there drinking a beer or a small Havana Club and Coke, while the rest of the staff take it in turns to collect glasses and come to the blind place to drink shots where they can be seen by everyone except the people in charge.

*

Dom is launching yet another new night, trying to solve the dead Wednesday that cannot be saved. Even Jordi Bone's hip hop night failed because he couldn't get the break dancers in any more frequently than once every few months. But Dom has a plan.

We get a delivery of a thousand round badges all with a Love Heart sweet on and the words **CANDY FACT**.

I hold one of them in my hands for a long time, looking at it and wondering who in their right mind would call a club night Candy Fact.

*

I'm having an argument with Karen. She's been sitting on the door till all night, sour-faced and silent. Because of her, there has been a horrible atmosphere in the place. As she follows me back to my office, I merely try to suggest that she might give a smile when people are coming in to spend their money in her nightclub.

"This is not a nightclub," she says.

I laugh, "It will always be a nightclub. There's nothing you can do to change that."

"You are living in the past."

I laugh again, and say, "You haven't got a fucking clue how to run this place. You can't even change a barrel."

And later, she comes to me again and apologises and tells me that I'm right.

*

It's the launch night of Candy Fact and it's also the first time I've seen Dom in this place after 9 pm. He can't stand still—he's either walking up to me and checking that I'm going to open the doors at 9:30 or going up to the bar, or up to his mate Aaron who is DJing this night as well as Desire on a Friday.

There are Candy Fact posters everywhere, the tagline —*playing the best bubblegum pop, hip hop, synth pop and kitchen sink pop. Upstairs is 50s/60s Motown tunes as punters doo-wop their way through the night.*

"What the hell is bubblegum pop?" I ask Aaron when he comes and asks for his rider for the night.

He shakes his head, "No idea."

Dom comes up to us.

"The Urban Outfitters people should be here at twenty-five past," he tells me for the eighth time.

I nod. For the eighth time.

*

We're standing looking through the glass in the entrance room. There is a sizable queue outside but only because Dom has bribed everyone by getting Urban Outfitters in to give away free goody bags to the first two hundred through the door.

"Remember," he says, "the pink ones are for girls, the blue ones for boys."

"Really, Dom? What about homosexuals? What colour do they get?"

By half past, the Urban Outfitters still aren't here and we walk round to the café entrance come fire exit and stand in the doorway looking down Gin Lane. Dom bites his nails.

"Come on! Come on! Where are they?"

"Late," I say. "Obviously."

"Well, why are they late?"

"Wardrobe problem?" I suggest.

The queue has grown to about fifty.

They finally turn up at quarter to, and I open the doors and get the queue moving. The Urban Outfitters set up in the room between the entrance and the upstairs bar where the kitchen is, handing out glorified party bags. Downstairs, Aaron is playing Tina Turner. Upstairs, Dom has made a playlist on Spotify that nobody is listening to. I hang around by the door till playing hangman with Shelly who has just played the word PREGGERS.

*

"How do you think it went?"

"OK, Dom. OK."

I'm pouring myself a drink from behind the bar because we have no staff beer until tomorrow. I've given the staff permission to do the same, and write it all down on the wastage sheet.

"Good. Well, three hundred isn't bad for the launch," says Dom.

"Do you want a drink?"

"Hopefully, we'll be able to top that and get a constant group in every week… erm, yeah, a ginger beer please…

but yeah, I've been speaking to Terry and Karen... and... erm..."

I zone his whining out after that, pour him his ginger beer and wish that he'd look somewhere else for a couple of seconds so I could spike his drink with something that might make him relax.

*

Jackson comes to my office after Cheese Night and asks if he can speak to me. I tell him to shut the door.

He tells me he wants to leave. He's had enough. He tells me he's written a letter to Karen and Terry and wants me to read it before he delivers it.

I tell him to send it to my private email.

*

For the attention of Karen Caines (and Terry Watson):

As (previously) required by my contract of employment (or the closest we have yet, or ever, had to it), I hereby give you one week's notice of my intention to leave the position of Bartender at Munks Club. I feel I am no longer suited to the projected working environment. Being a team player who relies on strong inter-colleague relationships, I fear that your apparent desire for a high staff turnover rate leaves me with little to no job security. I have therefore decided to move on and I've accepted a position elsewhere. This decision was terrifically hard to make. Three years is a long time, and certainly long enough to warrant a certain loyalty to the people you work with and the environment in which you work. My conclusion was made clear to me when I realized that without any security, without any trust (promises you have conspicuously failed to make good on so far)—my loyalty was shattered. There is, I'm afraid, no reward for working well at Munks anymore. We seem to be just as likely to be dismissed for simply not "liking" you as for any infringement of the (still yet to be finalized) contract of our service.

With this in mind, I cannot even comprehend promising (as employee etiquette dictates) that my last week will be one of energetic and vigorous fervour in regard to my duties. Nor will I consider raucous celebration, let there be no worry about that. As far as I am concerned, the situation is only depressing, and will be until you focus less on image and reputation and more on attending to the cogs of the machine you have been so animatedly attempting to sell upwards—or, no matter how many times you get a new staff base in, they will quickly learn to dislike your methods just the same as the last (a quick warning: the seeds of that style of dissent have already taken root).

I finish this letter of notice only hoping that eventually, you learn humility toward the experienced and efficient bar manager and workers (who, despite no doubt profuse protestation, you do **not** count as an instrument in your duet). They have had to see Munks Club dragged out of the gutter time and time again, to be dusted off and patted down and patched over. Without eventually listening to them, without accepting that sometimes you might actually just be **wrong**, then Munks seems doomed to fail and have that long-staved-off and haggard death finally catch up with it. That, most of all, is why I hand in this notice: I could not bear to stand by and continue working whilst you smother dead the last stirrings of what Munks could have been.

Yours respectfully,
Jackson Peters

*

The next day, I get an email from Karen telling me she's barring Jackson. I should reply asking her from which date he's barred, but I can't be bothered, so I put him on next week's rota anyway.

*

Listening to Slicer is like listening to a wasp stuck in a beer keg—he's only just started doing weekdays as he usually does the doors at another club down the road. He bounces up and down, animated, re-enacting his story with a demonstrative punch here and there at the invisible foe. From what I can decipher, this is what he says to me when it's just me and him on the door till for an early Thursday night gig—

"… and fuck me he was a huge fuckingfella you know about fucking nine foot tall, built like a fuckingbrick-shithouse, and he comes at me and says I'm gonna fucking slit your fucking throat and I say You can fucking try but I'm gonna fucking throw you out of here mate and he says

Try me you little cunt, and so I do and I grab the cunt and give him a couple of sneaky daps in the stomach, you know, and we're out of camera so no one can do fuck all, then I do a jab and grab and I've got him like this in a lock around the neck and he can't breathe and we open the fire doors and get the big bastard out of there and it's just meandhim out in the alleyway and he's still fighting, he won't give up, he's still wriggling and jerking but I've got a vice-like grip on the cunt, he's not going anywhere but the deck and I land on the cunt and take the breath out of him and he's panting like a fucking dog, and trying to crawl away and I stand up and let him before he somehow pulls himself to his feet, his t-shirt ripped and hanging around his neck like... like... whatthefuckdoyoucallem?"

"Scarves?"

"That's it, like a fucking scarf, yeah, and he's dragging a foot along the floor, waving his fists blindly, the cunt comes back for more and so I give him a few more upper-cuts to the kidneys, a few jabs to the arms, a left hook around the ear and then finally a fucking haymaker that sends the cunt down and he's not getting back up again part from on his hands and knees, when he crawls away like the fucking scummy cunt he is, and I've still got my high vis jacket on and barely breaking a sweat, I don't real-ise I've got blood over my knuckles till I get back in the club where there is some reallyfuckingnice fanny that have just walked through the door and I give them a good chat-ting up, the dirty slags, as they come in and..."

After a while, it's like listening to dubstep—every sentence has an endless drone and it all starts to sound the same.

*

It's Jackson's last shift. He wears his best blazer and green tie, pressed trousers and polished black shoes. He drinks shots with customers behind the bar, exclaiming "THIS IS MY LAST SHIFT!" and I turn a blind eye. Despite the promise in his letter, he works with more fervour than usual with Bret and Bran on the downstairs bar, dancing and singing along to the anthems of Cheese Night—'Stop' by the Spice Girls, 'The Winner Takes It All' by Abba, and 'ABC' by the Jackson Five—with the heart and frivolity of a man who knows he never has to do this again.

*

I've forgotten what fresh daylight tastes like because the only light I know is the one that occupies that chasm between late night and early morning when the streets are dead.

*

One of my more enterprising members of staff has written the words **THERE IS TOO MUCH DRINK LEFT TO BELIEVE IN DEATH** on a scrap of paper and Blu-Tacked it above the left-hand till in the downstairs bar. I look at it for a long time, then I start laughing and laugh all the way back to my office where I don't stop but laugh even louder—maniacal, high-pitched, unhinged—but nobody can hear me in a place like this. Had they, it's most likely they would have thought the architect of such a laugh completely and irrevocably insane.

*

After hours, sitting around the usual table in the den of inequity, lapping up what's left in the cellar before a delivery tomorrow, passing a joint around because tonight I don't give a fuck. Tonight, I'm done. Tonight, I would let this fucking place burn down.

Daniel, as it turns out, is addictively easy to bully. Especially when drunk. He lets himself into it, with the schoolboy wink, stud earring, boy band hairdo and designer stubble. That and the endless bullshit chitter-chatter about every subject that often ends in ridiculous comments such as—"I couldn't take it up the arse, I've got problems with my bum."

Bret and Bran keep giving him dead legs and he keeps appealing to me for help.

I open one eye and ask everyone if they want a shot of Wood's Navy Rum.

*

The bar staff contracts finally materialise. It only took them six months.

Karen puts up a sign advertising 15-minute slots for people to come in, go up to their office, sign the zero-hour contract and discuss any issues they may have etc., etc.

Nobody is up there longer than five minutes, except Laura, who, for some reason, gets on better with Karen than anybody else.

On a quiet Monday, I'm next door even though I'm supposed to be working, having a quick half and sitting with Bret and Bran who have just had their meetings. They're looking through their contracts, and sniggering at this page:

ALCOHOL AND DRUGS

Consumption of Alcohol on the Premises

Unless authorised by management, employees are expressly forbidden to consume alcohol at work or bring it onto the premises. Any breach of this rule will be treated as gross misconduct and is likely to result in dismissal.

Drug Misuse or Abuse on the Premises

Employees who take, sell, buy or possess non-medicinal drugs during working hours or on the premises will be committing an act of gross misconduct and are likely to be dismissed.

Intoxication at Work

An employee who is under the influence of alcohol or non-medicinal drugs during working hours will be escorted from the premises immediately. Munks will take disciplinary action when the employee has had time to sober up or recover from the effects of intoxication. Intoxication at work will normally be treated as gross misconduct and is likely to result in dismissal.

General

All employees are encouraged not to cover up for employees with a drink or drug problem but rather recognise that collusion represents a false sense of loyalty and will, in the longer-term, damage those employees.

Employees who recognise that they have a drink or drug problem, or that they are at risk of developing one, are encouraged to come forward for confidential help. They should speak in confidence with their line manager or secure the help of a colleague.

"Well, chaps," I say, "do either of you have a drink or drug problem you want to talk to me about?"

Bran is rolling a joint under the table.

"Yes, I do," says Bret, "I'm addicted to smoking ping pong balls."

We laugh.

"Tattoo Paul has a mate he was in rehab with who was actually addicted to smoking them," I say.

"Yeah, I know," says Bret. "I was speaking to him about that the other week. The guy started smoking them in Vietnam."

I look back down at the contract and think of the many years of drug abuse and inexhaustible excess that Munks has seen—the bar staff doing bombs of speed behind the bar to stay awake for another 48 hours, DJs doing lines behind the DJ booth, managers taking coke in the office. I've only ever sacked two people and that was because they were arseholes, not because they were drunk or drugged up.

I hand Bret back his contract, "I think we're all at risk of developing a drink problem working in that place. At least they got that right."

*

I ask Karen and Terry where my contract is and they tell me they're still working on it.

*

I haven't always been the manager. There was a time, years ago now, when I was just a humble bartender—life was simple, easy, carefree. I remember one night, it was a Monday and it was quiet, I was working with Bran on the old upstairs bar—a cheap and crappy thing compared to the shiny expensive one that Karen and Terry have replaced it with. I'd been on a five-day bender and wanted to sleep so I lay down on the floor behind the bar. Next thing I knew, Bran was kicking me and I could hear Ian, the then owner, talking. He leaned over the bar to look at the till or something—I could see the stubble on his neck and I closed my eyes.

If he'd looked down then and seen me, I would have been sacked, I'm sure.

This would still have all happened but it wouldn't have happened to me.

If only.

*

Summer brings bad business for a place like Munks. Most of the students go home, which means we lose most of our staff for a few months, the drinkers dry up and the takings go down. The new owners know it. Their plan?—to help out and do some bar shifts themselves.

The only night that stays busy is Cheese Night.

It is with a building sense of foreboding that I look at this week's rota and see the names TERRY and KAREN written in on Cheese Night when the place is full of the students who have stayed in the city, and those who have come back home from other universities, all of whom care about nothing but getting slammed and finding someone to share their bed with until morning.

*

The place is packed and I'm upstairs putting change in the till. I hear a random guy say to Terry—

"Can I give you a quid for a shot of Sambuca?"

"Erm, how much are they?" says Terry.

"I don't know—you work here."

"Yes, so I do… erm, Bret, how much is a Sambuca?"

"Two quid."

"Two pounds," says Terry.

"One quid for cash."

"I'm sorry, I can't do that, young man. I'd get in deep trouble."

"But aren't you the owner?"

Terry laughs, "I am indeed."

*

"How was it?"

Bret puts his head in his hands, his trilby hat off for once, his hair stuck to his forehead—"Excruciating."

Bran is chain-smoking two cigarettes at a time—"Never again."

Inez can't even smile, something I've never witnessed before—"Fucking sheet."

Even Daniel has nothing more to say than—"Fuck that. I can't do that."

"Well, you'll be glad to know that we had just over 300 through the door so you all still have jobs, for the moment."

I've never known it so quiet in the club. You could hear a termite sneeze.

"The worst part," says Bret, "was Terry with the soda gun. He'd put his glasses on to find the ice bucket, take them off, put them on again to look at the buttons, take them off again, then put them on again to find the button on the till… take them off, and then put them on again to find the right customer…"

"Well," I say after a while, "at least they didn't stay for a drink afterwards."

*

and it's the first really busy night for months, some of the old pissmakers and Munks/Bellhop legends are in town and the drink is flowing like it will never stop. Desmond and Marshall (the other two members of the infamous Slugs) are in with their retinue, the Cocktail gang of the city's swankier bars, Madsen is on fine form, playing records like 'Bam Bam' by Sister Nancy and 'No Diggity' by Blackstreet featuring Dr. Dre, and before I know it, there's a DJ-off going on upstairs between Madsen and Harry D who has turned up out of the blue with his Apple Mac and headphones having just finished DJing in a bar down the road, he wears a baseball cap, large round-eye style spectacles, a white Adidas zip-up jacket with blue stripes, and matching bottoms and trainers

when at half-past one, I'm called to the downstairs bar to deal with a guy who is kicking off at Georgie because he thinks he's been short-changed

then to the cellar to change the gas—it goes off just as I'm undoing the bolt and it spins round and round and round like a fire hose set off, scaring the shit out of me and I have to smoke three cigarettes in the cellar before I can go back to the club where

somebody has blocked both the Gents' toilets and I stand there with a bin bag over my hands, pulling out someone else's shit which has been expertly squeezed into a pint glass and jammed into the pan

and I bump into a very hammered Cub by my office and she hugs me and shows me her lighter that has a picture of the Eiffel tower on it, and she is apologising over and over again because she's decided to leave Munks and go and work next door in The Bellhop, and I say, "That's ok, I understand"

before I head to the cloakroom where some arse is refusing to move from the hatch because he thinks that Tattoo Paul has replaced his *genuine* and *very expensive* Superdry Windcheater with a fake

when a fight kicks off on the dance floor and a man's nose is broken and a girl has blood running down her leg, and Mike and Sam and Abasi have to drag a guy from the club who has ripped his shirt off and is telling everyone around him that he knows who they are and he's going to fucking kill them in their beds with a hatchet

and the battle upstairs has been lost and won and I take the till and wonder how Bret and Freddy Maytal have gotten so drunk, their grins are so big, their faces so pumped

and finally, it's the end of the night, the bouncers and DJs have been paid, everyone stays for more drink and more and more and more and more and more

until the well is as dry and as black as their souls and I'm closing all the fire exits as a new dawn fades

*

I'm short-staffed, Karen and Terry are on holiday, and despite everyone complaining to me about not getting enough shifts over the difficult summer period, I'm two people down on a Saturday and have to get Cub to come over from next door to help for a few hours, but even that isn't enough and I ask Daniel if he has any mates who might want to work.

"Yeah," he says, "my mate Little Harry."

*

Meet Little Harry, about five foot five, he wears tight black trousers, derby shoes, a baggy V-neck top that must have been meant for a woman, rosary beads, a pork pie hat and geek glasses. I put him on the door till and he sits down, customers already coming in, and Bret tells him what to do before disappearing back to the bar. After the night is over, I think *do one, Karen,* and offer Little Harry a job.

*

A daft but endearing drunk couple are making snow angels in the dust and dirt on the dance floor. I've seen them here before. I've seen them all here before.

It is Empire and it is dead. Barely fifty through the doors, the epitome of summer, so I shut upstairs at midnight. Bret and I are standing by the arch, he's telling me that a pretty dark-haired girl in white jeans came to the bar earlier and asked him for a cork to play a game called Ibble

Dibble with her friends, the drunk couple who've finished their snow angels now and are pulling each other around the dance floor to 'Fire' by Kasabian, and even though he knew we didn't have one, he went to look anyway. He says he really hated coming back and having to tell her no, sorry, and offering a smile. And then later, he tells me the girl from the drunk couple came up to him and said, "Callie really likes you, you should talk to her", and he's nervous now but trying to play it cool, as Callie, the very pretty brunette, comes up to us, acting confident but timid in the way she keeps looking down at the floor, blushing slightly. I take my leave but watch them from the bar where I serve a few people drinks, and when Bret comes back, he has a huge infectious smile on his face and I begin to ask myself if I'm too cynical when it comes to love.

*

Dom makes a fuck-up one Saturday and I find myself with no DJ downstairs. Madsen is in with his much younger wife (who apparently Bran once kissed at school, though I don't know if I believe him), sipping drinks in the upstairs bar. He looks quite smart for once, wearing a shirt and shoes. I go up to him and ask if he'll DJ downstairs tonight for £150 and his wife says yes.

The first incident of the night is his wife getting into a fight with a group of people in the upstairs bar when Madsen is asking Freddy Maytal if he left his records behind the bar. The bouncers think Bret's joking when he says there's a fight upstairs because there are only five customers, but we run through to see Madsen's mad wife pulling another girl's hair, and although I'm pretty sure Madsen's wife started it, I throw the other girl out and feel guilty for it. Her friends then leave in protest and we're down to zero customers. Then Bran comes in, hammered, with his mate Winston, orders two Jägerbombs and two pints of Guinness at the bar without paying and falls off his stool.

Less than zero customers.

The next thing that happens is Madsen's wife runs past the door till in tears and disappears out into the night. Stacie and I are looking at each other, wondering what the hell is going on, when Madsen, his shirt untucked and creased, appears with an unlit cigarette between his lips.

"Where's that mad woman gone?"

"Erm, outside," we say.

"I won't be long," he says and disappears after her.

Then Mike appears, shaking his head. "Fucking hell. Did Madsen's missus just run past?"

"Yep. And then Madsen, he's gone after her. What's going on?"

"Well, I was walking through the club and I happened to look up at the DJ booth, which seemed to be empty. So, I went up to it and looked down to see Madsen on top of his missus, finger raised, saying—'Shut the fuck up, shut the fuck up, you mad cow,' so I backed away, thinking, *uh oh, domestic*, keep well away."

"Well hopefully they'll sort it and he'll be back in a minute."

When the song downstairs ends and nothing else comes on, I send Mike out to look for them, and go downstairs to put the same song on again.

Not that there's anybody here to dance to it.

*

The old guard is dwindling—first Jackson, then Harrison (although he is still Karen's golden boy because he's in a successful band now touring the states). Shelly is next when she falls pregnant with my predecessor's baby and is bullied out the door under mysterious circumstances. Freddy Nelson has gone home for the summer but is coming back because he failed his third year at uni, split up with his girlfriend Leah who didn't and has gone home for good. And now... Jeremy's days seem to be over—demoted to the cloakroom when Tattoo Paul isn't around, his shifts cut down to two or three a week, he gets wildly drunk in the upstairs bar, cider free-flowing into his white mug, pronouncing, "Anybody for more tea?" in his weird high-pitched little voice.

A week later, Karen (who now goes through the rota after I've done it and makes changes) only gives him one shift—a measly three hours on a Cheese Night in the cloakroom. He fails to turn up, and shouts at her from across the road like a pissed-up queen, pointing, rambling in tongues... and when I go next door for a pint a week later, he's the one serving me.

This is what happens in a place like this.

*

and summer ticks by and we have no good weather in this godforsaken country and, even if we did, I would never see much of it anyway because my body is on New York time and all I see is the night. The band that Karen manages, a group of likely lads called Pre Nup Meeting, arrive and liven things up a bit, staying in the flat above The Bellhop and recording their new album in Munks studio. I take a picture (the first in years) of them leaning against the railings outside the café along with a few staff—Georgie, Bran, Freddy Maytal, Bret with his new girlfriend Callie—they're all dressed in shorts and t-shirts, sunglasses on, looking young and cool and hip, smoking roll-ups and smiling in the rare sun, seeming like they belong on a beach in LA, anywhere but here in this broken propaganda of a city, where it is inevitable that

the Pre Nup Meeting boys all become locals in The Bellhop for the month they're here, Cub starts sleeping with the drummer, the guitarist with Georgie, and the lead singer comes onto me one night at 4 am when we are the only two left conscious in the flat above The Bellhop after a lock in. Most people are passed out, in various states of drunkenness and undress, and he and I are left drinking warm bottles of Bud borrowed from downstairs. I ask him what he's doing as he goes to take his top off, his hands have already undone my belt, and he stops, apologises—we both laugh, light a cigarette, and finish our warm beer, and I

71

stumble out into the lukewarm daylight that has aged me twenty years in the last two. I look in the mirror when I get home, wondering why he thought I was gay, but I realise that it doesn't really matter because I have no sexuality left—it's gone, along with everything else I had, once upon a time

*

A rare night off, and on a Friday of all days. I almost wish it was a boring Wednesday or something then I could have stayed in and watched crap TV and eaten my own weight (which isn't much, admittedly) in Salt and Vinegar Twirls and Maltesers. Karen is in London with the Pre Nup Meeting boys, and Terry told me he'd look after the place and do the cashing up, which, in layman's terms, means the club will be managerless for the evening.

I go to the neighbouring city with Marshall of the Slugs who tries his very best to share his mildly expensive cocaine with me, but I refuse, only drink more, pub crawl until the last train back, where I spend the entire journey asleep in the toilet. I only wake up when my phone starts ringing and it's Marshall calling from the other side of the door, telling me to get my fucking shit together because we're nearly back, and I open the door and see he has a black eye and a split lip, his pork pie hat wonky. We get a taxi at the station and, as we're heading uptown, he tells me that some guy stole his hat and wouldn't give it back, so things came to blows. I pay the driver with the wad of cash I find in my pocket and we go to The Bellhop.

I walk out a few hours later with a blank memory, stumble the short distance across the street and let Marshall and myself into Munks through the studio door. We go down the corridor and through the door that's behind the upstairs bar—I stand and blink and Bran says, "You two look fucking hammered," and I duck under the flap and fight my way to Shot's Corner, where we meet Bran and the three of us do a shot of Tuaca that makes my thirst for more drink insatiable. Sometime later, I'm hanging onto the downstairs bar and giving back the money I've just been paid in exchange for very large Havana Clubs at "staff" prices.

And then, for some inexplicable reason, I'm sitting in the same place I have sat for the last thousand nights, around the table with the rest of the staff after the night is done, and it's around six in the morning, two hours after closing, all of us trollied, me bulldozed, I miss every other step as I make for the Gents' and realise with a sudden horror that Terry is still in the office. I poke my head in, eyes wide, bloodshot, estranged and see him—tiny like a child in the office chair, surrounded by piles and piles of money that he doesn't know what to do with, staring at an empty cash sheet.

He looks at me, desperation in his eyes and says, "Help."

*

73

I wake up fully-clothed cradling a bottle of Havana Club.
Empty.
A husk.

*

"And here is a lovely picture of our manager surfing on the bonnet of Bret's car in the early hours of this morning."

All sorts of hungover. My head is full of broken pieces of the night, the morning, and the day after—events that have no order, no emotion, no meaning. Every cigarette I smoke comes back up. Every drink I smell makes me drunk again.

The staff are chuckling as they pass Georgie's iPhone around. Finally, it comes to me. I rub my eyes.

"It's a good picture."

*

a night off that I book as holiday every year, and I'm boycotting Munks, determined not to go there, but equally determined not to spend the night sitting in my flat alone and staring at the walls where pictures used to hang, and so I take the short walk down to The Bellhop and spend my evening downstairs in the cellar bar. A few hours later and I'm already starting to talk gibberish, already starting to lose my mind. Bret, Harrison and Will, the old promoter who now lives in New Zealand and isn't a cock like Dom, have joined me and we're doing shots of Tuaca and after every shot, I order four more and we're playing spoof and I'm losing, badly. Around us, the place is filling up quickly and Dave Abbott is DJing and playing songs that I've never heard before. I'm talking to Will about his new life in the Southern Hemisphere, and he asks about how the new owners are doing and we all laugh. Then I'm asking for four more shots and Cub holds up the bottle which is empty—I can see right through it to the calendar on the wall that tells us it is September 11th

exactly ten years ago today, my father died in the south tower when it fell

*

Morning comes. The time on my watch says late afternoon. I wake on the sofa, running through the base emotions that have no names and are only dead feelings. The flat is a state. Harrison is asleep on the other sofa, still wearing his beanie hat. In the middle of the room are empty bottles—Havana Club, Grey Goose, Jack Daniel's, and a bottle of champagne (a Lanson Black Label), the one we'd been saving for her birthday. I look through the pile of bottles at the stains on the carpet, too crippled inside to move, too scared to check my sent messages because even now, at a time when I can't even remember my own name, I can still remember her number.

*

Bouncer talk—you need an ear of iron and no heart to listen to it. You can't understand it unless you have stood on the doors at night.

*

THE DOORMEN

Early evening. Outside Munks Nightclub.
THE DOORMEN are lurking, hyena-like,
occasionally preying on the very slow stream of
customers coming in by asking them for ID.

PETE BONE
> So, Sam, who was that girl you took home last night?

SAM
> What girl?

PETE BONE
> Come on, don't be coy—who was she? Tell Mike about her...

SAM
> Who?

STACIE
> The one we saw you with.

MIKE
Has he been taking fat girls home again?

PETE BONE
Looked like, what do you call it? Norbert.

STACIE
Norbert?

PETE BONE
Yeah. You know, that film with that annoying black prick in it who does all the parts. She was a huge, big fat black girl. Wearing a short yellow thing. Absolutely fucking disgusting.

STACIE
Fucking hell, Sam.

BILL
You'll fuck anything, Sam.

SAM
Fuck you, Bill, at least I did fuck her.

PETE BONE
So you did fuck her?

SAM
No.

PETE 2
> Don't you have a missus?

SAM
> Well… yeah. Sort of.

MIKE
> What do you mean… sort of?

PETE BONE
> Poor girl.

PETE 2
> You disgust me, Sam.

SAM
> I didn't fuck her, alright.?

PETE BONE
> Well, why was she in your car when we drove past you?

SAM
> Was giving her a lift home.

MIKE
> Where?

SAM

To my house.

PETE 2

And?

(SAM looks embarrassed and his whole face, including his overly large ears, has gone crimson)

PETE BONE

Ha, now it comes out... come on, Sam, did you spread those fat arse cheeks?

(They all wince and groan and laugh at once)

SAM

Well, she got in my bed, naked, and starts stroking the headboard, which is like green velvety stuff.

PETE BONE

Why do you have a green velvet headboard?

SAM

Well, not velvet, sort of like a golf green.

PETE 2

You mean a bowling green?

SAM

Yeah, that's it. Well, she starts stroking that with one hand, lying on my bed, fingering herself

with her other hand and I look down and see her
thong has got caught on my foot.

PETE BONE
    And how big was it? Like a fucking pair of
    granny pants?

SAM
    Too big, I could have worn it as one of those big
    bikini man things.

STACIE
    A mankini.

SAM
    Yeah.

MIKE
    What colour was her thong?

SAM
    Green.
    (They all groan and wince and laugh again)

PETE BONE
    Fucking horrible. And then what? You fucked
    her?

SAM
  No. I just stood there at the end of the bed. She's
  moving and moaning, and then I take my trousers down and have a wank.

MIKE/PETE BONE/PETE 2/STACIE/BILL
  What?!

PETE BONE
  You dirty bastard.

SAM
  Yeah, so I just toss myself off, come, and pull my
  trousers back up and she says is that it and I say
  yeah and I can smell her from the end of the bed
  it's so fucking wet.

BILL
  It's so wet you can smell it?

MIKE
  Yeah, how does that work, Sam?

SAM
  You know what I mean, and then, after I've done
  that, I tell her that's all she's getting, and make
  her put her clothes back on and then I give her a
  lift to the bus stop.

MIKE/PETE BONE/PETE 2/STACIE/BILL
(incredulously)
    To the bus stop?!

SAM
    Yeah.

BILL
    What time was this?

SAM
    About 6 in the morning.

BILL
    Such a gentleman.

MIKE
    But don't you have a missus, Sam?

SAM
    Well, yeah. But it's not cheating, is it?

MIKE
    How?

SAM
    I didn't fuck her.

*

Meet DJ Tim, a pale, meandering and aimless sort of fellow, a big Spurs fan, who wears a snapback cap with the letter T on it. The wrong side of 35, he wears white t-shirts that do nothing to help his permanently pallid complexion and he can talk shit until his tongue rots. Like Madsen, he DJs with old-school vinyl. He's been in this city for years, and Dom has got him in to DJ a few nights every now and then. Annoyingly humble, two pints of cider down him and he spends the entire night apologising to me when there is nothing to apologise about.

*

"The fucking idiots are going to fall off."

Mike and I are outside—we've just opened the doors, and we're watching a group of lads standing on the rooftops opposite. They are laughing, waving, wearing shorts and rugby tops, some even still have their sunglasses on. They hold up cans of Carling—the secret juice of their potvaliancy. They sit up there until it gets dark. The club remains dead until midnight so we stand outside, waiting to see if one of them is going to fall off.

*

Business picks up and Karen hires more staff, including Lizzie, a friend of Georgie's who I first meet when she stays for a lock-in. She has a loud drunk voice, says she has an interview with Karen tomorrow and is asking for advice.

I'm trying to take the downstairs tills and all I want to do is tell her to shut the fuck up. But when she's sober, she isn't so loud, and I find out that she's lacking a bit of substance upstairs (in fact quite a lot) but makes up for it with a smile, and for some reason all the boys find her attractive.

*

Meet the reprobates. They wear skinny jeans and denim jackets and All Star American-style sneakers with fraying laces, tight hooded tops with the zip undone and striped shirts tucked in with battered DCs, Chelsea boots and trilby hats, pork pie hats, flat top feather hats, knitted beanie hats with leather jackets with tight t-shirts picturing some underground band they saw at a gig years ago, long maxi dresses with cardigans with the sleeves rolled up and spotted scarves and dark leggings with denim shorts and shredded back sweaters, and light faded seam tank tops and chunky Doc Martins to kick your face in with baggy low hung jeans with brown leather belts and key chains, and snapback caps with their jeans turned up at the calf to show the tattoo that they should really regret but never will.

*

Meet the guy wearing ripped jeans and a tight t-shirt with the words **PREVENT TEEN PREGNANCY, FUCK A**

12-YEAR-OLD written on it. He is about seven feet tall, standing on the pavement next to the front door and giving a war cry.

Mike and Pete Bone, their gloves already on, take a fighting stance.

But just as it looks like the paedophile is about to launch at the doormen, Karen, who has been sitting on the door till all night (and is directly responsible for the awful mood the bouncers have been in), steps between them.

She spreads her arms and shouts—"WALK AWAY!" and begins moving towards the guy. "WALK AWAY!"

Mike and Pete look at each other in bewilderment, then at me—"What the fuck is she doing? She's gonna get fucking clobbered."

"She's fucking mad," says Pete Bone.

I'm already calling the police.

By some miracle, Karen comes out of this unscathed. No punches are thrown, the police turn up, the paedophile calms down and goes home quietly.

*

Karen and Terry hire more staff, including a twenty-something bonehead called Phillip to manage the café. I stay out of it—in the last conversation I had with them, I made it clear that I would remain doing the club nights but I didn't want anything to do with the café. They also advertise for a fancy chef, well beyond their budget, and end up hiring Tattoo Paul (who used to do the odd shift in the kitchen next door). The menu includes a long list of 'no-fuss finger food'—Pieminster Pies, fish finger sandwiches, burgers, chips. They do a special night when all the staff are invited to come in and try it and we all come (even some of the bouncers) to get free food. It's almost friendly. I bring up a crate of staff Coors beers. The food is good. They've almost convinced us it could work. And then we remember that this is all madness.

*

"WHAT'S YOUR NAME?"

Early on a Friday night, Madsen is playing '54-46 Was My Number' by Toots and the Maytals too loud, and I'm covering Bran whilst he goes next door to score some weed.

"CRAIG," I say.

"NICE TO MEET YOU CRAIG," says the girl wearing a Nirvana t-shirt with a picture of the baby from 'Nevermind' on the front, black leggings, boots, and too much eye makeup.

"LIKEWISE," says Craig.

"NICE SUIT," she says.

"THANKS, I LIKE TO MAKE AN EFFORT FROM TIME TO TIME."

"IS IT TRUE THAT ALL THESE BANDS PLAYED HERE?" she asks when Craig brings her the double Vodka and Coke she ordered along with her change.

"YEAH," says Craig.

"COOL," says Nevermind Baby Girl.

"WICKED," says Craig.

She smiles.

Craig smiles back but after a few seconds, it becomes forced because she won't stop staring directly at him.

Repeat, and replace Craig with a name of your choice.

*

Late one night, I am up in the offices that Terry, Dom and Karen use, high above the club, beyond the recording studio and the many locked rooms. Karen is in London, the staff have all gone home, I am alone up here using the big, expensive printers that Dom uses for posters because mine has packed up downstairs. Something is open on Terry's desk, a legal document, and my eyes are drawn to this sentence at the bottom:

**You cannot use the premises or the building
for anything illegal or immoral.**

*

The café does well for a few weeks—pulls in a few tourists and the odd wayward local on his way for a pint next door, and early evening is not a bad time when the bands are eating after soundcheck, a couple of guys play acoustic guitar while the sun's still out, and you can take a seat at a table on the slabbed pavement above the road and have a smoke with your sunglasses on to hide the weariness.

Phillip proves to be almost competent, although it is clear that he has no idea what sort of direction Terry and Karen want to go in because as the opening day fades away and customers dwindle and the days darken and nobody comes through the café door and the staff eat all the food, the fact is as clear as it ever was—people don't want to eat food in a place where they got drunk the night before, made a fool of themselves, and went home with a stranger.

*

Pete Bone is IDing girls on a Cheese Night.

The first approaches. He looks at her ID.

"Very nice, come in." Gives it back to her. She smiles and enters.

The second approaches. He looks at her ID.

"Very nice, come in." Gives it back to her. She smiles and enters.

The third approaches. He looks at her ID.

Gives it back without saying anything.

Her face falls. She almost trips on the way in over the threshold.

Mike and I hang our heads. We can't look. We want the ground to swallow us up.

*

I pin an email I've just received to the wall by the door till. And along the top of it, in big red letters, I write—
EMPLOYEE OF THE MONTH.

SUBJECT: PETE BONE

Dear Manager of Munks (sorry, I don't know your name, but I hope I have contacted the right person to deal with this issue)

I was in Munks Club last night (Tuesday 27th) and unfortunately at the bar was a very drunk man causing upset to my friend and I. We had asked him to leave us alone, which fell on deaf ears, hence me seeking help from the bouncers. Initially, I pointed him out, and was told they couldn't act on my word—they had to see him misbehave himself.

So, after the man continued to be an annoyance, Pete Bone came and very calmly escorted him outside, and then came back to my friend and I to check that we were OK.

Not only am I astounded at how kind and polite and genuinely decent all of the bouncers at Munks are, but I was also touched at how brilliantly Pete handled the situation.

I hate going to all the other clubs due solely to the arrogant and abusive bouncers.

I am probably telling you everything you know already, but I assume they don't get enough praise (people are normally happier to make the effort to complain as opposed to thanking them).

So, many thanks as always for employing the best bouncers I've met, but also a great thank you to Pete who couldn't have dealt with last night's issue any better.

Kind regards,
Chloe Lee

*

Terry and Karen have told me I work too much, but I bet they're only saying that because my hours have been going up and up and up since they started because nobody seems to know how to do a damn thing around here. Tight bastards won't even put me on a salary. And now I've been told to take some time off. Apparently, I'm looking tired, thin, gaunt. Karen recommends a holiday in the country, so I ask her which one and she doesn't even smile.

*

Meet Blanche, or Barry, depending on how polarised your views are. She is a regular, a nice guy, and appears most Friday nights, sitting in the upstairs bar, tapping along to the music with his painted red nails, knee-length black boots, hair loose around her shoulders, drinking pints of Guinness and black. She puts a hand on Bran's arm whenever he brings her a fresh pint and says, "Thank you, my flower," and laughs.

*

I'm talking to Jeff about Dom.

"Ooh, don't get me started on that little twat," he says.

I snigger and light a cigarette. We're outside. Jeff has his trademark black rucksack on (although, after all these years, I still have no idea what he keeps in there) and is just about to go for his usual walk around town (doing whatever he does) after sound-checking the bands, before coming back a few hours later to put them on.

"Fucking useless," he says. "Wouldn't know hard work if it bit him on the bollocks. Have you seen the way he sends Tanya running around after everyone, doing everything?"

Tanya is the new music rep—chirpy, Vietnamese, a good worker, makes things run smoothly on gig nights. Things have been strained between Dom and I for months, mainly due to his inability to tell me how much the bands are supposed to be paid. Tanya is solving this. I'd rather deal with her than Dom any day.

"Hasn't got a fucking clue. And he's never here."

"I think I've seen him in this place once after midnight," I say.

"That's right, the lazy bastard. I can't believe Terry has put him on a salary."

"He's *what?*"

"On a salary. Sorry, me duck, I thought you knew."

"No." I put my fag out on the wall behind me. Bastard. The wormy prick. "Do you know how much?"

He exhales, "Not far shy of twenty, I think."

"Cunt."

"Aye."

"What the fuck does he do apart from putting a few posters up?"

"Not a lot, me duck."

*

For the rest of the night, I'm in a foul mood. It's a Saturday and girls keep coming up to me and complaining about things and I ignore them all and tell Freddy Maytal and Bran to deal with any problems and if they can't then come and get me in the office, but only if it's a real emergency, and only then if the emergency is that the place is on fire.

I turn the computer on and look at some new shoes online, smoke a cigarette and then another.

Dom.

On a fucking salary.

Bastard.

I look at the newest Google searches but immediately wish I hadn't.

cool gap year rucksack

audio described film

do you ever forget your first love

Who the fuck is doing this?

*

At the end of the night, I go straight for the staff vodka and pour Mike and myself a larger one than usual and we sit straight down with the staff. For some reason, Freddy

Nelson is here, just back from home, absolutely fucked. Tanya is here too, slightly tipsy, hiding any nervousness with cigarettes and her deep and rather rough voice. Around a quarter to three, she says she better call a taxi, but I tell her to stay, have another drink. Then add,

"And we're all going to start talking about how much we like Dom."

Bran laughs. Daniel sniggers.

Tanya says, "Oh my god, want to hear something funny about him?"

"What?"

She smokes her Marlboro Light, held elegantly between long fake painted nails, and sips a Vodka Coke. "A friend of mine went out on a date with him last year."

"Really?" says Georgie, "Do we know her?"

Tanya shakes her head, "No, she lives near Dom. But apparently, they went back to his, well, his parents' house after the meal, and he put Barry Manilow on."

"Oh god."

"Yep, and then, from somewhere, god knows where, he pulls out some snakeskin."

"Snakeskin?" says Laura. "What a fucking oddball."

"Yep, and then he starts rubbing it on her leg, saying things like *do you like that? Do you want some more?*"

We're speechless, put our fags out in the plastic cup with a tiny bit of water at the bottom. There's a series of small hisses before we all start laughing like loons and I fetch a fresh crate of beer. Then Freddy Nelson falls backwards off his stool and lies on the grimy floor, looking up at us, until he points at the stool he's just fallen off, a silly grin on his face, and for some inexplicable reason, exclaims:

"BROWN SEAT!"

*

I cash up the next morning, still drunk.

*

We're in the pub the next day talking crap, and at various intervals, one of us will shout "BROWN SEAT!" and we'll all laugh, a crackpot cabal hiding in plain sight.

*

Dom takes Bret, Georgie, Daniel and Laura to the Freshers' Fair to promote the new café.

I text Bret—*How was it? x*

Alright. Dom is a douche. x

I text Laura—*How was it? x*

OK. Although Dom is a dick x

Later, Bret and I are outside smoking after setting up both bars early for a gig—some band called Mumford and Sons are playing and we've sold lots of tickets.

"Mate, it was so funny. The four of us kept rubbing my leather jacket on the chair behind the stall and saying—is this snakeskin?"

I laugh.

"He was oblivious, kept telling me and Daniel off for just chucking stuff at the freshers and saying 'free shit'."

"That's what freshers want."

"I know. He stood there, spouting all sorts of spiel." He puts on a voice that sounds uncannily like Dom—"*Hi there—have you heard about Munks? No?—well, it is a live music venue and...* it was like Karen had him learn the speech by heart. It was the same every time like he'd been rehearsing it in the mirror."

We smoke, both thinking the same thing—can you rehearse this?

*

Freshers' week. Every night we have a queue at the door, students stumbling in, wearing all manner of stupid clothes, in all manner of states, wielding the booklets that were handed out at the Freshers' Fair, asking for the special £5.00 Pieminster Pie and a pint of Coors meal deal and waving the voucher in my face. I have to explain to everybody that we don't serve food at night, they have to come back tomorrow during the day. They say fuck off they're going to Wetherspoons. I'm glued to the door till except for when I have to keep running downstairs and back to fill it up with change, watching the parade of drunken youths in fancy dress— three tigers with no beards, Spider-Man without his mask, Snow White missing her dwarves, Borat, Donkey Kong, Superman with the outline of a large penis drawn down his inner thigh, cats, dogs, bears, and bunny rabbits. Towards 1 am a plump girl holding a silver rod, with her face painted yellow and gaps in her teeth so they stick out, appears at the door. Pete Bone says, "What are you supposed to be, love?" she says "Pikachu!", screeches, and smacks him on the arse with the rod. We all laugh and let her in, and Pete says, "She's a feisty mare."

*

It's the time of night when I'm closing the café door to open up the club door, but there are lots of people already in—populating the upstairs bar with carefree chatter, the early evening drinkers out enjoying the last of the summer nights that occasionally make an appearance in the first week of October. Dom is also here doing some work for a change. Bret and Bran are on the bar (Bran's eating his packed lunch that his mum sends him to work with) and we're listening to feel-good classics like 'Lovely Day' by Bill Withers and 'Get Up I Feel Like a Sex Machine' by James Brown, and Bret's girlfriend Callie is here too with Cub, both of them tipsy, Callie talking about what she and Bret did in the summer, tales of their courting—breaking into the Botanical Gardens down by the weir at 3 am after a night out to sit on a bench together, eating pizza, holding hands and watching the moon on the water. And then the bar is filling up with the casual weekenders, and Madsen is in playing his usual reggae and funk, and Dom is still hanging around, now talking to Callie, puffing his chest out and talking in his most professional manner about this band and that band, and the big one that he's getting in for New Year, the name of which he can't possibly disclose—but then he splutters and doesn't know what to say when she enquires, sweetly, "So, are you the poster boy?"—and I have to hide around the corner until I stop laughing.

*

It's my first holiday since I can remember. Terry has just about learnt how to cash up by now and there are no nights coming up that will be difficult to manage, like Dead Pulse/Kick (dubstep/drum and bass night), not that I care, so I take it and run. Well, not far. I watch TV long enough to realise that there is never anything good on and that Ant and Dec will outlive us all. At night, I can't sleep and have to drink myself into a slumber with whatever's left in the cupboard, which isn't much at all. I manage to avoid Gin Lane until the Tuesday night when I think fuck it and go to The Bellhop for a drink. On the way past Munks' Café, I see Karen putting up fairy lights in the windows and don't wave. Then that first pint turns into a hundred and I spend the rest of my holiday there, eating vegetarian food, going home at intervals to sleep and sober up. I'm never usually sober or even awake enough to read, but Bret has lent me *Less than Zero* and *Imperial Bedrooms* and I read them in the daytime, sitting on the faded red leather sofa by the window, watching the snow, and listening to all of Elvis Costello's albums with Cub (now the assistant manager), and when it gets dark and busy, I come out of my corner to try and be sociable, mind full of depraved and soulless characters, and I stand at the busy bar and order a large Havana Club, take a sip and look around and realise I've been reading about my life because, although the decades change, there is always another lost generation.

*

Dom's Candy Fact night has gone from strength to strength. It has failed to make any money since the opening night and I don't know why he's even bothering with it anymore. He gets the Urban Outfitters back in for an end-of-term special, giving away more goodies, and less than fifty people turn up. At eleven o'clock, he goes home to bed.

Exit Pegasus—the saviour of Munks.

*

Some guy called Devlin is playing and Tanya is running around like a headless chicken, and there are hordes and hordes of underagers in (we give those of drinking age wristbands) and big private security guys hang around, following this Devlin chap everywhere. Tanya has been sent down to the shops by Dom for a bottle of Jack Daniel's and lots of other stuff for Devlin's rider, and all the 16-year-old girls are going mad, and finally, when he comes on, the venue is packed. Mike and Pete Bone stand facing the audience on either side of the stage until they're ushered out of the way by the bigger security guys, and I go up the stairs and stand outside for a while, smoking, wondering what all the fuss is about.

*

Meet the middle-aged woman crying her eyes out at the door till. She is wearing a sash saying MISS PRUDENT and has emptied the entire contents of her bag onto the counter.

"Oh, here's the manager," says Lizzie.

"What are you doing?" I say to the woman.

"I need my coat."

"Where's your ticket?"

"I can't find it."

"Then you'll have to wait until the end."

"But I really need it."

"I'm sorry. Club policy."

I roll a cigarette. She stamps her feet.

"I really, really, really fucking need my coat. I'm going to London tomorrow… please."

I ignore her, apply the finishing touches to my cigarette then look out the door. Summer is long gone, the days have drawn in—how cold is it outside tonight? Should I put a coat on?

"Please! I am a mother."

I go outside without a coat.

Inside, she continues raving, making Lizzie go through the contents of her bag again, then again, then again— before storming back into the club.

"What's she kicking off about?" asks Stacie.

"Lost her cloakroom ticket."

I look up and the night is clear enough to see a thousands stars. I wish I'd put a coat on.

*

Ten minutes later, we're running downstairs because, on the CCTV screen behind the door till, we've just seen the same woman vault over the cloakroom door and attack Georgie. Miss Prudent is kicking and screaming, grabbing and slashing at coats, wild and unhinged—until we drag her out. She slips to the floor and starts wailing, hammering the ground with her fists. Her MISS PRUDENT sash is lost.

*

An hour later and she's still sitting in front of the cloakroom. The downstairs DJ is playing 'Bad Romance' by Lady Gaga. Fifteen minutes ago, I lost patience and Mike called the police. She stares at Stacie and me like we've kidnapped her children and occasionally lets out a little moan, her lipstick smudged.

When the police arrive, she gets up and leaves straight-away, telling the officer about her mistreatment. We follow her upstairs, shaking our heads, and within thirty seconds of being outside, she has a cigarette and the coat of a stranger who holds her hand and listens to her sorry tale of injustice.

*

Daniel comes to me in a panic and says there's a guy at the bar who has just ordered thirty-two Jägerbombs.

"What's the problem?"

"What?"

"If he wants thirty-two, give him thirty-two."

"We don't have that many shot glasses..."

"Find some, beg some, steal some from next door, I don't know—improvise."

"OK."

Ten minutes later, I go up to investigate. Daniel has found enough shot glasses and the guy who ordered them, some smartly dressed dude in a suit without a tie, is lining them all up into a Jägertrain. Then he stands at one end, flicks the first shot glass, and we watch them all drop like dominoes, barely making a splash.

*

I've just opened the doors on a Cheese Night and nobody has come in yet, and Mike gestures me over to where he and Stacie and Dave 2 are standing by the railings outside the front door, giggling around a phone.

"What's up?"

"Look at this picture," says Dave 2, giving me his phone.

It's Sam, with his shirt off, oiled up, with his arms thrown up in a pose around his head.

"What the hell is he doing?" I say.

"He sent it to me today," says Dave 2. "It's his photo to go with his application to be a male escort."

I crumple with laughter.

"He's covering his ears!" says Mike.

"In case it puts women off," adds Stacie.

"The worst bit," says Dave 2, "is that the stupid twat is paying to join this company."

"How much?"

"About a grand, he said."

"Is he in tonight?"

"Should be here any minute."

When he turns up, he can't work out why we all keep throwing our arms up around our heads to hide our ears. As the night goes on, even the customers start doing it to him, but he just stares, chewing his gum, and we're none the wiser as to whether the penny has dropped yet.

*

A month later, he's still waiting for his first date.

*

Kick night, drum and bass, music I can't make sense of, no matter how much I'm forced to listen to it. I'm outside, blending into shadows amongst the smokers, when a guy in a white t-shirt, jeans and black shoes comes out and says—to no one in particular, anyone who will listen—"You wouldn't believe how many drugs I've shifted in there tonight!"

He laughs, grins, lights a cigarette. I finish mine, go inside and have a word with Mike and Abasi.

When the guy tries to come back in, grinning, eyes red and wide, Abasi stands in front of him, blocking his path, shaking his head, and Mike says, "End of your night, mate."

"What? Why?"

"You know why, and whilst we're on the subject, you are barred for life. Now get the fuck out of here before I get the police down."

We fight the war on drugs one idiot at a time.

*

I know from experience that going out flyering is a love/ hate sort of activity. On the one hand, you have to walk the streets on a Friday or Saturday night, handing bits of paper to people who don't want them and just throw them on the floor or put them in the nearest bin. But on the other hand, it is common knowledge amongst the staff that if someone is sent out flyering, they are going to end up in a pub, drink for an hour, probably put the flyers in a bin themselves, then head back up the road to Munks when it starts to get busy, well on their way to enjoying the rest of the night serving the juice mob. I don't have a problem with it—just as long as they don't come back absolutely battered.

However, now Dom has taken it upon himself to hire Flyer Girls and pay them a pittance to wander the streets between 9.30 and 11.

I'm outside the café door having a cigarette and making a mental list of what I need to do before opening when I notice two scantily clad and nervous-looking girls hanging around the other entrance. I have no idea why they have so few clothes on. It's December.

"Can I help you?" I ask them.

"We're here to see Dom," one of them says. They are both shivering.

"Flyering?"

They nod.

"One second."

I pull my iPhone out and ring Dom's office upstairs.

"Munks Live Music Venue, Dom speaking, how can I help?"

"Flyer Girls here to see you, Dom."

"OK. Tell them I'll be down in a minute."

I gesture for them to follow me through into the club, tell them that Dom will be down soon, then leave them standing by the upstairs bar which is dark and empty and waiting for Bran to come in to set it up. I go downstairs to my office to do some work but only end up going on the

internet, looking at the Google searches and scratching my head because new ones have appeared and I'm starting to doubt my own sanity:
how to argue properly
my hairs falling out
woman hired hitman to kill husband

*

I go back upstairs half an hour later, after clearing the Google search history and starting next week's rota, to find the Flyer Girls still there, looking cold and very bored.

"Are you still waiting for Dom?"

They nod. Too timid to be pissed off, too cold to cry.

"Fucking arsehole."

I find him upstairs in his office, sitting at his computer playing Words With Friends.

"Dom. Flyer Girls. Downstairs. Waiting for you."

He jumps to his feet.

"Sorry, I was just finishing some work."

We both look at the screen. The last word he played was INEPT.

*

A few days before Christmas, Terry has an exclusive night, a private party for his friends and family. Paul makes a big pot of curry and we ship it out to people in cardboard containers. Terry's wife sits quietly in a corner with a few old greyheads, sipping gin and tonics with a mineral water in between. His daughter is sloshing around, spilling champagne, holding onto the arms of a dozen different men, saying in a loud voice every ten seconds, "It's ok, honey, Daddy owns this place…" before coming up to the bar and ordering round upon round without paying a penny.

Karen is nowhere to be seen. Terry told me earlier she'd been called to London for some sort of emergency.

Around 9, the man himself comes up to me and Freddy Maytal at the bar.

"Right—Freddy, we're going on in a minute, I need a bottle of red and a pint of water on the stage by my keyboard."

"No problem, Terry."

He scuttles off.

We look at each other. "Ever heard Terry's band?" he asks.

"Nope."

"What are they called?"

"Only Fools and Horses."

"Seriously?"

*

Half an hour later, we're standing at the top of the steps to the dance floor, crippled with laughter, watching Terry, who is wearing a pair of Stevie Wonder glasses, dancing behind his keyboard, sometimes doing little jumps in the air with his hands raised.

*

Christmas Eve. Sitting in the waiting room at the doctors', staring at a poster that says **Catch it, Bin it, Kill it,** trying not to be sick, hoping I can hold on, gripping the seat with both hands to keep my face straight, as inside my kidney pulsates. There are five other people here. I can't look at their faces. I get up and walk to the water dispenser, drink three cups, and feel better already, more human, breathing steadily again. I'm staring at nothing, through the glass into the corridor which leads down to the consultation rooms, when I hear a voice I recognise. Madsen is standing at the desk with his two little daughters, both dark-haired like him. I hear him say, "They both have sniffles but their mother thinks it might be cancer." The receptionist doesn't know what to say. I'm just glad that I didn't have a mouthful of water because I'd have spat it everywhere. I sit back down and stare at the poster again.

Eventually, Madsen walks into the waiting room, his kids run off to the play corner, and he sees me, and takes the seat beside me.

"How's it going, chief?" he says.

"Not bad."

"What are you in for?"

"Headaches."

My name is the next one to be called, and he winks at me and wishes me luck, and I walk past his kids who are causing a scene as they fight over the same toy, and I follow the doctor's footsteps, walking in his shadow, but before we get to his office, I hear Madsen say, "Stop messing around, you two, or you'll wake up with nothing but coal in your stockings tomorrow morning."

The doctor shuts the door behind us and we both sit down. Then he asks me the same questions he did last time—*Have you been suffering from any shortness of breath?—Have you noticed any loss of appetite?—Have you felt any increasing need to urinate at night?—Itchy skin? Muscle cramps? Nausea?* And my answers are always no, no, no doctor, my kidney feels fine, everything seems okay, and this time luck is on my side, because my blood pressure is normal, and my weight is the same, which means the questions stop.

I put another mint in my mouth. The doctor writes something down and says he's renewing my antirejection medication. Then he stops writing, looks at me, and says with cold eyes that have seen it all before.

"I'll see you in another six months."

*

Standing outside with Dave Abbott, a haze of smoke and white breath hangs over the queue which stretches all the way along Gin Lane, a good two hundred yards long. It's the first Cheese after Christmas and every year it's the busiest. I'm also short-staffed, have only two up and two down, and will invariably spend a lot of the night helping behind the bar downstairs. I go and stand on the other side of the street and take a picture of the queue on my iPhone. I come back to Dave and say, "Shall we send it to Dom?"

"Ha! Yeah—with the caption: THIS IS A REAL CLUB NIGHT."

*

The next day, I find out why Karen left for London in such a hurry—from Dom, of all people.

Her band—the Pre Nup Meeting—they've decided to sack her as their manager.

"But don't tell anyone," says Dom, giving me an accusing look. We're standing in the café sorting out what's happening on New Year's Eve. "She's really upset by it."

*

I don't say a thing but obviously, I'm not the only person Dom tells, because a few days later I'm sitting in The Bellhop with Bran and Bret and Callie, and we're listening to 'Let's Go Surfing' by the Drums and it's snowing outside—Callie is wearing a big thick coat, scarf and gloves, and Bret's got his arm around her and still she's shivering.

And Bran says, "Is it true that the Pre Nup boys have given Karen the boot?"

"Who told you?"

"Cub."

"Ah." I forgot she was friendly with the drummer. Maybe Dom is a loyal minion?

*

a hellish night, the dreaded night, the one to ruin them all—
New Year's Eve, where we stay open until 5 in the morning,
Dom has booked a member of Biffy Clyro to DJ, and we
charge twenty quid on the door. There's a steady stream of
celebrities through the door all night, such as Dougie from
McFly, half the cast of Hollyoaks, and Peter Crouch and
some other footballer Mike tells me is an Icelandic hard
cunt called Herman Hreidarsson. But he's very pleasant to
me and they both buy me several drinks early on, however,
as much as I'd love to get hammered, I stay sober all night
because someone has to, running around like a loon after
everybody else, clearing up sick and blood and booze

until we finally throw all the customers out and shut
the doors and I tell Bran to get the absinthe out, while I
go upstairs to pay Madsen who is getting almost £400 for
a few hours work, only to find he's already gone and I hear
laughter, a boy's and a girl's, and see Dom, who perhaps
for the first time in his life has had something other than
ginger beer to drink, pulling Georgie through the upstairs
bar hatch, through the door to the corridor, and up the
stairs that lead to his and Terry's office

walk back downstairs thinking that strange things
happen on New Year's Eve in a nightclub, to find Madsen
smoking a joint with Bran and Little Harry and the Biffy
Clyro DJ at the tables. I notice the band door is still open,
with about five random girls in there all totally naked and
playing Twister, and somebody has made up about fifty
lines of cocaine on the shelf by the sink and left them
there, and they're all laughing because there's a guy dressed

as a chicken collapsed on the floor by the door leading out into the street. Bran has left the bottle of absinthe unopened on the table by Jeff's sound desk, so I collect it on the way to my office where I sit down, open it and swig from the bottle whilst I cash up

and by the time I'm finished, I'm seeing faces and insects and ghosts, the office is covered in mist and I've only just noticed that somebody has written **HAPPY NEW YEAR PRICK** on a post-it note and stuck it to my pinboard

look at my watch and somehow it's only 7 am—it feels like I've been here for days. Stand up on wobbly legs and go out to the club to find Madsen, Bran, and Luke from next door with their shirts off, taking it in turns to give each other nipple cripples. Lizzie, Little Harry, and Jackson (like some Shakespearean tragic hero back from the dead) are sitting down laughing at the round tables which are stacked with empty bottles of beer, and I turn to them and say, "What the fuck is happening?" and they can't answer, but they don't need to because strange things happen in a nightclub on New Year's Eve, the likes of which we shall not speak of again

*

I'm haunted by a phone number that I can't forget no matter how drunk I am.

*

Meet the well-dressed, skinny guy who always tries to get in late on a Friday night when he's had too much to drink. He wears a black trilby hat and an Abercrombie jacket and will usually stand outside late in the night, constantly pestering the bouncers to let him in, refusing to take no for an answer. I've threatened to ban him lots of times but he doesn't take any notice. "Can I come in?"—"No."—"Why not?"—"You're too drunk."—"Go on."—"No."—"Go on."—"No."—"Please."

And so on, for hours, every few weeks, time and time again.

Every so often, people will come in and he'll spot his chance and try and sneak in behind them, only for Pete 2 and Mike to put an arm across and stop him, "Listen, mate, you're not coming in."

"Why not? I'm not a bad man. I'm not a violent man. Please."

"You're not coming in."

Then he'll fall back, stand out in the street again and wait. Sometimes this goes on for an hour or more—every so often, he'll come forward again and lean on the doorframe for another round of the same thing. "Can I come in?"—"No."—"Why not?"—"You're too drunk."—"Go on."—"No."—"Go on."—"No."—"Please."

After almost an hour of this, he comes forward again and says, "Please, I'm really thirsty, I want a drink."

Pete 2 looks out at the empty street and says to him, "Do you want a drink?"

His face lights up, he nods his head keenly. "Yeah, I really want a pint."

"You want a pint, do you? Here you go then."

And from behind his back, Pete 2 produces a pint of water which he throws into the man's face, giving him a little push at the same time. He falls backwards into the street, sits up and stares through the door at us like a lost child. The bouncers snigger. The guy splutters and looks like he's going to cry. Water drips off his hat, off his chin.

"What did you do that for?"

"Mate, you've got to be careful," says Pete 2, "it's slippery that step."

He rubs his face, and slowly, dejectedly, he walks away, his upper body stiff in the cold.

Pete 2, looking guilty, turns to me where I'm sitting on the door till. "Sorry," he says.

I shrug, "I always thought he could do with a good wash that chap."

*

and we have the staff Christmas party in late January, an event that I dread and hotly anticipate. I sort out a deal with a friend who manages a bar down the road, and on a dead Sunday we all go to the café (amazingly it still exists after five months) for a free curry cooked by Tattoo Paul, a couple of liveners, before we leave Karen, Terry, and Dom, and go onto The Bellhop for a quick shot of Sambuca, then onto my friend's place called The Tankard where I put two hundred quid behind the bar that Terry had (very surprisingly) given me before we left Munks. When that runs out, I do a whip and get a tenner each from everyone, and we drink more and more—Hand Grenades (a shot of Jäger and a shot of Goldschläger jammed into the top of a tumbler with a splash of Red Bull in the bottom—you have to pull the plug to drink it), and Mexican Hand Grenades (substitute the Goldschläger for Tequila). Tattoo Paul and I go to the bar and order a couple of Death Grenades (add a shot of Bacardi 151 to the standard Hand Grenade) and then pour the Bacardi 151 (75% ABV) into the bottom to sit disguised amongst the Red Bull, and then give them to Bran and Freddy Nelson who's already falling around like a hoodlum, yelling REVVING and GOD YEAH and BROWN SEAT, and Tattoo Paul laughs and drinks his cup of tea, and for some reason, somebody is talking about Pimm's and Little Harry says he can't drink it because it sends him mental and so somebody (probably Bran) orders him a Pimm's, and from this moment on we all call him Harry Pimm's. I order a Death Grenade for myself with a champagne chaser and drink it and then have a word with my mate the manager and put another hundred quid behind the bar out of my own pocket and order another few Death Grenades that cost a tenner each and take them over to the only two bouncers who came, Mike and Pete 2. When my hundred pounds is all gone and drunk, The Tankard is shutting and we're all trying to leave, Freddy Maytal has to take his girlfriend home, who not half an hour ago asked me for a job and I said yes even though I have no power at Munks anymore, and she thanked me and said she hated working at another club down the road because they are all pricks and I said that we're not much better, and then Freddy Maytal has to ring Bran's mum because Bran has fallen asleep on the sofa after getting off with Lizzie who is almost as fucked as he is and we all need to leave but he won't wake up, and I'm told by Bret that Bran smoked a joint outside and it's knocked him for six, and we get him outside and sit him down, leaning against the wall, his Sideshow Bob hair damp with drink, his dap shoes muddy, his jeans around his thighs and his chin on his chest. When his mum turns up it takes four of us to get him into the car, and then, now only half our original number, we go to a shit club down by the river, but it's the only place open, and I pay for everyone to get in and prop the bar up and the next thing I know, Mike is dancing on one of the poles on the stage, and then Tanya is doing her own very professional routine that has everyone asking questions, but I suppose she is a dance student. The last thing I remember is Freddy Nelson falling over on the dance floor before he's dragged out for being too drunk and then we all have to leave because they're closing, but I've left one last shot of Tuaca undrunk till now and I tip it back and everything dissolves into orange-tainted black

*

Holed up in the cloakroom chatting with Tattoo Paul because there's nothing better to do and because he has lots of chocolates and good stories. He draws my attention to some new writing on the wall.

"It appeared after Bret covered me for a fag," he says, chuckling.

BRAN SHAT ON HIS MUM'S BATHROOM FLOOR AFTER THE STAFF PARTY

*

"Why did you tell anyone?" I ask Bran a day later in The Bellhop. It's been a week since the Christmas party and he's only just drinking again.

"I don't know," he says. "Just don't tell anyone else."

"Too late," I say, "it's all over Facebook."

"Fuck sake!" He finishes his drink and goes out for a fag. A minute later, after laughing for a while, I follow him.

*

Late on a dead Saturday and DJ Tim is asleep on the sofa downstairs. I've already paid him after I shut the upstairs bar at 3 o'clock—his signature was shaky when he signed the receipt, chatting absolute bollocks about his ex-girlfriend, his pool league, his cat, fucking mother's maiden name, and father's favourite LP. He's had four pints of cider and his head drops until his chin is resting on his chest. He wears a New York Yankees basketball vest.

Hidden around the corner behind him are Mike and Sam. Mike appears, holding a cup of ice. They begin putting ice cubes down DJ Tim's back, sniggering, grinning, like schoolboys.

Soon all the ice is down the back of DJ Tim's vest. He tips his head back, still asleep, and his cap falls backwards exposing his forehead.

Sam walks past and slaps it.

"FUCK OFF!"

DJ Tim wakes up, looks around, stunned, before going back to sleep, forehead still exposed and slightly red.

Then Mike walks past and slaps it again.

"FUCK YOU!"

This time he leaps up, eyes wild, taking a fighting stance, his thin frame comical underneath the baggy clothes. Then he sees Mike and Sam laughing and straightens his cap and feels the wet patch on his vest.

*

There's only so long you can do this job.

My predecessor lasted two years.

His, only one. And hers less than six months.

I've managed this place for three years now and can't help feeling I'm on borrowed time and the reaper is coming for me.

*

There are lipstick marks on the pale green wall of the Ladies' toilets—hundreds of them, some smudged, some faded, some clearer than others, some with names written next to them—**EMILY—PIPPA—SARAH—LAUREN—LAURA T.** I stand there one day, looking at the wall. The staff are making a racket in the downstairs bar because there was a delivery today and I ordered a crate too many of staff beers, and I think somebody should take a picture of this, put it in a gallery and call it **THE SLUTTY WALL.**

*

Closing time and Blanche is the last one out, all over the place, one high heel lost, makeup smudged, wig at an angle, slurring, eyes spinning in opposite directions. He collapses in the entranceway. Bran says she's been drinking neat Bacardi all night, tossing it back and telling him that he can take her out anytime he wants to. Now her skirt is hitched up around his armpits and we can all see the stockings and suspenders and a hairy chest. Pete Bone is pretending to be sick in the corner. The other bouncers stand around, sometimes staring, sometimes looking away. Nobody knows what to do. Nobody wants to touch her.

I decide to take some responsibility and step forward. "Blanche…" I lightly slap her face. Rouge comes off on my hands. Long eyelashes flicker. "Wakey, wakey, Blanche. It's time to go home. Bran is going to take you back and ravish you."

The bouncers crack up.

Mike gives her a shake—"Wake up, Barry. Bran has something for you in his pocket."

After ten minutes of this, we give up because we run out of innuendos and all our laughter has dried up. I look at Abasi and Sam and say, "I don't suppose you boys fancy picking her up and carrying her to a taxi? I'll give you a staff beer."

"No way, man."

"Fuck off."

I sigh and take my phone out, and curse the world that it has come down to me to tell the police that we have a drunk transvestite in our doorway.

*

Some girl who slipped down the stairs last month is trying to sue us, so, after a brief discussion with Terry, I introduce a spillage report sheet and tell the staff to fill it in a few times a night if they see any large puddles that need attention. Blizzie (aka Black Lizzie—this is what we now call her and it is in no way racist because she started it) comes up to me when I put a sign up detailing all of this information, scratching her head and says, "But, how do we know where all the spills are?"

I tell her that the foundations of the club rest on an old molehill and that I am able, by looking at a very old document that details where all the moles entered and exited, to predict where customers are most likely to spill their drinks.

"What? Really? That's clever."

I nod, solemn.

*

In my office, I have a box full of identities. I find them after most nights, on the floor all over the club, outside in the street where the smokers gather, under the bench seats in the alcove by the stage. Hundreds of them.

It's just a pity I can't find my own.

*

Stacie, Pete Bone, and I watch a really fucked guy feel his way along the wall, stumbling and slipping, trying to find the exit in the dark. He's wearing jeans, an expensive jacket, brown Diesel boots and mirrored Ray-Bans.

"What the fuck is he doing?" says Pete Bone.

The guy trips and goes to ground.

"He's out of his fucking head. Why is he wearing fucking sunglasses, eh?"

The guy gets up, his sunglasses slanted. For some reason, I feel like I recognise him but I can't think why I would.

"Fuck this, I'm throwing the drunk prick out."

And we watch Pete Bone approach the guy and tap him on the shoulder. Just as Pete takes one of his arms, I realise why I know the guy, and it seems Stacie does too because he's backed off, saying, "I'm not getting involved with this, fuck that," and I'm running over, and Pete is getting forceful because the guy is shouting that he's not drunk, he's blind, he's fucking blind, but Pete doesn't listen. He says, "Whatever mate, whatever... you're pissed, get out," and then throws him through the fire exit. And I'm there too late, standing beside Pete Bone whilst the guy pulls himself to his feet, swearing, his sunglasses broken, and in the light of the fire exit, I can see him properly and realise that it's some famous blind writer called Grant or Greenwood or Galloway or something.

"You fucking twat, Pete, the poor guy is blind."

"What? He is? Well, it's too late now, I've thrown him out. He should have a fucking white stick, shouldn't he?"

I smile at the guy, who is brushing himself down, and then remember he can't see my smile, but he can probably hear everything we're saying and we may be in deep, deep shit.

Then Kyle puts 'Straight to Hell' by the Clash on, and, for some reason, the guy starts smiling, laughing, and then he pulls out a cigarette and feels his way up the three or four steps that lead to the road.

*

The café is dying. Phillip has moved on to a real job and everything is in limbo. It's no longer open during the day, only early evening. The kitchen has failed—Tattoo Paul tells me he threw away almost all of their produce last week because it was beyond its use-by date, and we're standing smoking, talking about how everybody could see this happening except them.

*

The club stays busy—well, not as busy as it has been in past years, but they're just about still making money. Laura and Inez leave, but I have a good core of staff that I'm happy with and I move Tanya from Dom's skivvy to doing the door till. Karen seems to have lost interest in bringing in new blood, in fact, she has lost a lot of her drive since the New Year. The last thing I remember her doing is putting up the fairy lights in early December and, in the first or second week of February, making a pig's ear of putting a band name up on the café wall after they'd just played. She decided to write **RUN FOR TRAINS** in permanent marker and not with paint and a stencil like a normal human being. The once regular and excruciating staff meetings have all dried up and she spends more and more time in London. She doesn't even bother interfering with the staff rota anymore and leaves it all down to me. I look down at the list of staff I now have and think—faces and names change, but everything stays just the same.

*

I wake up with a text on my phone from Jinx the cleaner telling me there's a smashed round table on the street outside the café and one very broken window that it came through. I check the time of her text—8:59 am.

I look at my watch. It's almost five o'clock in the afternoon.

*

An hour later, when I've woken up properly, dressed, had lots of tea, cigarettes and something to eat, I get a text from Karen.

Meet at Cafe. 7 sharp.

Then Mike texts me—*Just got an odd text from Karen.*

Me too.

What do you think it's about?

Well, I had a text from Jinx this morning about a table that's been thrown through the cafe window. From the inside…

Oh fuck

*

Before Mike and I can say anything, Karen pushes two pieces of paper across the table towards us.

"What's this?"

"Your written warnings."

"Why?"

Karen looks at Terry, "Well, it seems that last night after Empire, a customer was locked in the venue."

Mike and I look at each other.

Last night… I try to remember it.

Mike did his usual check at about 2:30—there was just staff left, and then about an hour later, I locked up as usual and left with Bran. Nothing amiss.

Mike is shaking his head. "I did my usual check, usual time, there was nobody here but staff."

I'm nodding, "And when I left, usual time, knowing that Mike had done his final check, there was nobody here."

Karen shifts slightly. Terry is looking at his hairy hands.

"Well," she says, "we have looked at the CCTV footage and it seems that at around 3:45, there was a man still in here. A man wearing a kilt. A man who was somehow missed when Mike did his *final* check, and who was then locked in the venue."

She looks me in the eye.

I want to slap her.

"And this same guy threw the table through the café window to get out," she says.

Terry coughs. The corner of Karen's mouth twitches. Mike looks at me and I shrug, stand up, leave the written warning on the table, walk out and light a cigarette.

Outside, I blow smoke out over the railings and look down at the road, at the litter in the street waiting to be cleaned up.

*

Want to know what really happened?

*

At 2:34, Mike does his usual final check and then leaves. There is nobody in the club who shouldn't be there. Then, when the manager is in his office along with Bran, who he's giving a lift home, Kyle, and another DJ mate of his leave at 2:57 via the usual café door that turns into a fire exit on club nights. That is when a guy who has just left the club, dressed in a kilt and with blue face paint on, comes back in through the café door that Kyle has left open, stumbles around for a while, goes downstairs and falls asleep under the round tables where the staff usually sit after hours. At 3:28, the manager walks from his office to the switch panel by the downstairs bar and cellar and because the place is in darkness, he doesn't see the sleeping Scotsman. He and Bran leave via the usual exit. He doesn't set the alarm because it's been playing up lately but he locks up.

Around 4:45, the sleeping Scotsman wakes, disorientated, still pissed. He stumbles around, goes behind the bar and stands there for a while, lifts his kilt up and pisses in the sink. Then he goes upstairs, stands behind the bar for two and a half minutes before picking up one of the round tables and throwing it through the café window.

*

Mike and I put all of this together after closing up, the same day we were handed our warnings, sitting upstairs in Terry's office and going through the CCTV footage. And then, the next morning, we both come in, climb the stairs back up to their office and tell them that we're not accepting our warnings.

Karen is shell-shocked—her mouth opens, then closes again. "What… why? You can't… we've already explained…"

Terry looks curious and says, "Hmmmm."

Dom makes a small, strange noise like a frog being stood on.

"We would appreciate it, bosses, when things like this happen, if you would go through the CCTV footage in a bit more detail."

We leave our written warnings on the desk when we leave.

*

Freddy Maytal (whose girlfriend Vickie now works here too) and Bran go out for a drink with Karen on a Friday night they all have off. Freddy tells me that when she's not around this place, she's like a different person.

"Totally laid back," he says. "And she's quite good fun, she likes a drink."

They all come in at about 2 in the morning, fucked. And when I go to my office, I find Karen in there, sitting at my desk, going through my emails. I stand in the doorway, watching her—she doesn't even know I'm here.

*

"Well, I understand you're not too happy about this."

"No, I'm fucking not. It's well out of order."

Terry and I are downstairs in my office. I called him away from Karen to tell him about his business partner's pissed-up nocturnal antics.

He stands in the doorway, scratching his almost bald head. His face is red.

"As I said, I understand…"

I wait for him to say something else.

He sighs, "Look, just try and keep this under wraps. Don't speak about it to anyone but me and trust me when I say that I'll sort it."

*

A week later, a rumour begins to circulate that Karen is leaving Munks. Notices appear throughout the club giving details of her departure along with lots of other sentimental bullshit, but nobody reads it properly and we all just wait for her to be gone.

*

"I'm going to leave the day-to-day running of the club to you," says Terry. "I will be here during the days, as usual."

"OK," I say, resisting the urge to point out that the running of this place has always been down to me.

We're upstairs in his office. All traces of Karen have vanished. He sits behind his big desk, turning on his swivel chair like a kid, chin barely above the top of the table.

"I have meetings planned in the next few weeks with a few potential investors, so all going well, there will be more money to spend soon."

"On what?"

"Oh, you know, getting the café up and running again, new bar downstairs, a lick of paint here and there."

Is he fucking mad?

"Right. And staff?"

He nods, hands clasped under his chin. "I trust the workforce you have got in. I also think you know the sort of people we want to work here."

"OK."

"You will of course need to train a few existing members of staff up so they are able to manage the place, which will also give you the capacity to take a few nights off a week."

"OK."

"It's up to you, but I suggest maybe black Freddy and the guy with the hat."

"Bret."

"Yeah."

*

Dom has bought a smoke machine and had it hooked up to the ceiling above the dance floor where all the flashing lights are. He comes to me and asks if I can fill it up for him—he's too small to reach up and tip in the liquid.

*

Meet Chucky, drug hound and superstar DJ who still lives with his mum (a few houses down from Bran's mum), just back from Ibiza where he's spent the last year trying to make it in the big time. This obviously didn't go to plan as he's back home and asking me for a job. I give him a bar shift for old-times' sake, but after a few shifts, he fucks up and drinks too much, so I sack him but he's already wrangled a regular DJ night from Dom who likes him for some reason.

*

Some ginger-haired chap called Ed Sheeran has caused fifty adolescent girls to queue outside the club since some-time early this morning. I walk past them shortly after 9 am on a change run to the bank. They stay there all day until I open the doors at 7 pm, and the place fills up with kids drinking Cokes and lemonades, milling around the stage until the man himself comes on shortly before 9.

"Heard of this guy?" I say to Vickie on the door till.

Considering she's going out with Freddy Maytal—a man who has a permanent smile on his face—there are times when I wonder if she is capable of such a thing as a smile—she sits on the door, stamping people's wrists, reading a book and looking like she's just been told cancer is eating her insides. It must be a work thing because when she's not here she doesn't look half as grumpy.

"Yeah, he's quite well known I think."

"Right."

"Oh, and some guy called Newton Faulkner just came in—was on Ed Sheeran's guest list."

"Oh yeah—he's a singer or something, isn't he?"

"Yeah. He sang 'Dream Catch Me'."

She goes back to her book. I go outside to smoke and look through the window wondering if all of us looked that morose, would we have any customers at all?

*

Later, when all the kids have been kicked out and Empire starts, Kyle puts on 'Last Nite' by the Strokes, and Bret is in with Callie and her friend Jaz, a girl who I vaguely recognise—Callie tells me Jaz used to come in here all the time when she was a student. Jaz is insatiable about Newton Faulkner being here, tells us all she's in love with him, and follows him around everywhere like a puppy dog, talking to him at every opportunity, and he seems to be interested, a great big smile on his face, but that may have more to do with all the drink he's had rather than Jaz's conversation. An hour later, Callie, Bret and I are standing by the stairway next to the dance floor watching the two of them, when Newton Faulkner takes a tentative step back to lean on the wall, then slips down the stairs backwards and lies in a heap on the empty dance floor, his ginger dreads in a puddle of booze, still holding his pint cup and grinning.

*

Meet Fuming Willy—a Scotsman who grew up in Bournemouth, a music student who lives with Freddy Nelson. We call him that because he always looks like he's fuming, even when he's happy, even when he's sad, even when he's pissed—when, in fact, he looks even more like he's fuming. The tangled black hair doesn't help. I put him on the bar with Bran and Freddy Nelson on his first night, and he keeps his black beanie hat on for the whole of Cheese Night, barely breaking a sweat even though the place is rammed with people dancing to 'Call Me' by Blondie, and the ceiling is dripping.

*

Standing by the door till listening to Pete Bone and Mike crap on about football, Tanya is painting her plastic nails red on the till. The place is dead. Two chav guys and a girl who just paid to come in about a minute ago come back out, and one of the guys says to Tanya—"You could have told us it was shit in there, darlin'," and the other guy, the skinhead, says quietly but still audibly, "Or just fuck off back to where you came from, love."

And as soon as he says it, Stacie charges over from the doorway and the guy is saying, "Calm down, Stace," and the girl is saying, "Yeah, calm the fuck down, Stacie," and Pete Bone is saying, "Get the fuck out of here," and Tanya is giving the guy the finger—she's spilt her nail polish everywhere and is shouting at the prick who is being dragged away by his friends saying "Yeah, yeah, fuck off back to China," and she says "I'm Vietnamese, you prick!" and he says, "Same fucking place," before disappearing around the corner, and Tanya vaults over the counter and chases after him, screaming.

I watch her go, sighing. Stacie gives me a dark look and says, "Fucking hell" and Pete Bone says, "I wouldn't want her chasing after me."

"Hell certainly hath no fury like a woman scorned."

I get some paper towels to mop up the nail varnish. When Tanya comes back in tears, I tell her to take the rest of the night off, and she says thanks and gets her stuff, then says she's going next door to get very, very drunk. Stacie gives her a hug before she goes. Even Pete Bone gives her a smile and a pat on the shoulder.

The three of us watch her leave. Stacie mumbles something and goes to the staff toilets. Dave wanders to the door and pokes his head out.

What else should I have done? What do you say in a situation like that? Can you say anything?

I look down. The nail polish has left a dark patch on the grey surface.

*

Meet Andrew Gately—another music student and a part-time busker, tall with blonde dreadlocks and a baby-face. On his first shift, I convince him that the DJs are the Chemical Brothers because their song 'Galvanise' is playing and he says, "Really?" and I say "Yeah," and he runs off to text his girlfriend.

*

Post dubstep night and this place is a tomb of destruction. What is it about the people who like this music? They order a drink, go to the dance floor and throw it on the floor—there is no other explanation for the amount of liquid I have to squelch through at the end of the night. I pick up the coins that fell from their pockets, robbing the poor to feed the poor, as I go over to the DJ booth to turn off the sound system. When I flip the power switches off, it makes a noise that cracks your eardrums and all the staff groan and hold their ears. All except Freddy Nelson, back to his old ways after a time of calm and sobriety. He keeps shouting "BLAMMO!" and trying to successfully sit down on a stool, but after failing, he starts fighting with Bran. Fuming Willy and his girlfriend, Pinkie, are almost as inebriated—they were all in tonight getting hammered, with moving jaws and eyes as round as saucers. Willy and Pinkie are an odd couple. She's a very nice, but rather feral girl, who works in Urban Outfitters, and I'm not the only one to wonder why she's going out with a skinny, surly Scotsman who wears Doc Martens and rarely puts his hood down.

I walk over to them and lean on Jeff's sound desk, watching.

The club phone starts ringing.

"Someone get that."

Bran breaks away from Nelson and goes behind the bar to answer it.

He comes back.

"Chucky wants to know if he can come in for a drink?"

"Yeah, if he wants."

Bran disappears upstairs and a few minutes later, reappears with Chucky.

Freddy Nelson, now scrambling around on the floor, stops, looks up at Chucky and says—"CHUCHY!"

*

The lights have just come on at the end of Cheese Night and Blizzie comes to me to tell me that a girl is having a seizure in the toilets.

Pete Bone and Sam follow me to the Ladies' toilets where we stand over the poor girl who's wearing nothing but a skimpy dress, her shoes lost, her hair matted with dirt as she convulses on the wet tiles. Vickie and Blizzie are holding her hands, trying to talk to her.

"Maybe she left her tampon in too long," says Pete Bone.

"Pete, don't be a wanker!"

I turn to Pete, "That was too far, Pete."

"What?"

After a while, her convulsions stop and she is still. I check she's breathing then call an ambulance.

*

Walking through the upstairs bar, jangling keys, Euro Pigeon is playing 'The Boss' by James Brown (Madsen has disappeared to Thailand so he's become the resident funk DJ upstairs) and the night is just about to get going. Bret and Bran are on the upstairs bar, Fuming Willy, Little Harry and Freddy Nelson are downstairs, Tanya is in the cloakroom and Georgie is on the door till. Her and Dom are an item now so we have to be careful not to slag him off too much in front of her. Just last night, she stormed out after work because Bran called him a piece.

I pass the old red leather sofa opposite the DJ table and my attention is drawn to the right-hand arm. I examine it, then call over Bran and Bret.

We stand and look at it—the great big gouge in the arm that looks like a giant has taken a huge bite of the foam, the leather flapping like skin at the edges.

"People get hungry when they're pissed," says Bret.

*

I train up Freddy Maytal (even though he's moving to Brighton soon) and Bret so they can manage the place when I'm not here. I show them which key fits which lock, when and how to open and close the fire doors, how to replace the till roll when it runs out, how to take a Z reading from the tills and a final reading from the PDQ machines at the end of the night, how to cash up, how to read and fill in the cash sheet, how to open the safe to deposit the cash taken that night, and how to set the alarms when everything is done.

But I can't teach them how to deal with the drunks when they come at you, or what to do when you see someone walking through the club with a pint glass that shouldn't be here, one that they've brought in from next door, and even when you confront them about it, they plead ignorance, claiming that they're not aware of the unwritten law about not taking beverages from one establishment into another. It is impossible to teach them how to deal with everything that might happen in a place like this because drunks are unpredictable, and even they don't know what they're going to do next.

*

One night, Gately comes to me in a very excited mood because he's managed to get the word *chuchy* accepted into the Urban Dictionary.

*

1. Chuchy

a Chuchy is a person who obviously has a problem. He will just stare at you for no reason clutching his testes shouting Chuchy in his high pitched voice.

He is generally a piece. Often referred to as Touchy Chuchy.

Girl 1: saw you talking to that guy earlier
Girl 2: yeah he just came over to me randomly, he seems a bit of a Chuchy
Girl 1: yeah I see what you mean, deffinatly very Chuchy

Buy chuchy mugs & shirts

chuchy   cockpiece   cunt   bellend   wanker

by Chuchybasher

*

"Have you heard about Bill?" Sam says to me early on a Thursday, when a band called The Hawk Does Flyeth are playing and there are less than ten people in. It's Dom's fault—he only put one poster up for these guys, and admittedly they are awful, but I still feel for them—playing to an almost empty room, the bar staff, and the sound man.

"Yeah, he handed his notice in last week."

"Can't believe it—a traffic warden!" He sniggers. "He'll have his peak cap, and his thingy belt…"

"You mean utility belt."

"That's it. With all his gadgets on it—mobile phone, handheld computer thingy, camera… what else?"

"Walkie-talkie, torch…"

"Yeah."

"Umbrella."

"Really?"

"Yep. And a mousetrap."

"Why?"

"Mice like to hang around under cars."

"I didn't know that." He spits his chewing gum out into a paper wrapper. "And his nice uniform. I can see him now, stomping around town giving out tickets. Did you know he has to wear a stab vest?"

"It's not so different from doing the doors here, Sam."

He laughs, "I can't stop thinking about him in that peaked cap…"

I light a cigarette, wanting to tell Sam that maybe he should start looking for a real job like Bill. But then I realise a comment like that would make me a hypocrite.

*

Candy Fact has plummeted to new lows—constant poor turnout, no profit, Aaron no longer DJs and Dom has got Chuchy in to do it instead. It has now become Chuchy Fact. The only people who come through the doors are people who aren't allowed in anywhere else. I shut the upstairs bar at midnight. Chuchy plays whatever he feels like until 2 am and by then there are only a handful of people left to throw out.

*

Fuming Willy, Bran, Freddy Nelson, and I are next door having a pint and I say, "So what do we make of Gately?"

Fuming Willy gives his usual shrug and takes a swallow of Guinness. Bran says "He's alright", and Freddy Nelson frowns and says, "He's a bit try hard."

"But he did get Chuchy in the Urban Dictionary," says Fuming Willy.

"Yeah, he tried to get brown seat in too, Nelson, but they wouldn't accept it," I say.

Nelson sips his pint and looks confused, "Why does everyone keep saying brown seat?"

There is no answer to this except—"Brown seat!" which the three of us shout in high-pitched voices as Nelson looks on clueless.

*

I see Blanche in her daywear. No wig—his short, greying dark hair combed back, a two-day beard, slightly crumpled Moss suit with a boring grey tie, black shoes, briefcase, red umbrella. I'm standing behind him in the queue for the cashpoint. When he's finished, he turns and our eyes meet. I smile and say, "Hi, Barry."

"Oh… hello." He half stops, walks a pace, then turns back, holding his umbrella up. "Erm… Blanche wants to know if you can put her on the guestlist for later?"

I smile, "Tell her it's already done."

"Great."

He winks at me, before striding off through the puddles, into the building a little up the road with the words KNIGHT FRANK emblazoned on the window.

*

Some guy comes up to the door till and asks nobody in particular why there's a guy in the cloakroom reading Alcoholics Anonymous.

Mike, Vickie and I laugh.

"Who's in there?" asks Vickie, who I have dubbed the Smiler because it is something that seems to be beyond her.

"Bret," I say.

I go to investigate and sure enough Bret is sitting in Paul's chair reading the big book.

"Any good?"

He looks up—"Illuminating. Listen to this—*if when drinking you have little control over the amount you take, you are probably alcoholic. If that be the case, you may be suffering from an illness which only a spiritual experience will conquer…*"

*

I have a spiritual experience that very night. After we close, I drink far too much staff vodka and wake up on the sofa upstairs, with Jinx the cleaner tapping me on the shoulder.

*

"Which one of you fuckers keeps texting me?"

"What are you talking about, Chuchy?"

Almost five in the morning after a Saturday night and I'm all cashed up already because it was quiet and I shut upstairs two hours early, which is why Chuchy and Bran are pissed already.

"Somebody keeps texting me, saying they are some girl and shit."

"What sort of stuff?"

"Well—like this one," he takes out his battered iPhone which has a crack down the middle of the screen. "*Hi sexy, you are rocking the beats tonight. Keep it up.*"

We all laugh.

"You've got an admirer, Chuchy," says Tattoo Paul.

"And then this—*Do you fancy a shot big boy?*"

We all laugh again.

"Fuck off! Who is it?"

"Your mum," says Bran, and punches him on the leg.

"Fuck off, Andrew!"

They start tussling, a couple of schoolboys, soon rolling over the floor and knocking into chairs, then down the step into the bar.

"Who served Bran vodka and Red Bulls?" I groan.

"Sorry," says Little Harry.

"Don't. It turns him into this."

*

Freddy Maytal and Tattoo Paul have organised a ska night —SKAFACE, upstairs only, £1 entry, on a Monday night. Ambertones, Fuming Willy's band are playing and the place is heaving. Fuming Willy has removed his t-shirt and is showing off his withered-looking chest as he smashes the drums. I imagine him to have a Celtic tattoo on his back, but when he finishes and turns around to pick up his Guinness, I'm disappointed. Dave Abbott goes on the decks and plays ska and 2-step classics until close.

*

Meet Rick, a doorman who used to work here a few years ago. Now he's back from Thailand on a mission to make enough money to pay for his Thai bride to move over here. Mike has got him back to replace Bill.

He runs into the entrance hall, skids to a halt by the till and says, "Some cunt just told me he's gonna fucking kill me."

Mike, Pete Bone, Pete 2 and I follow him down the stairs to the bar where Rick points the guy out—he's about seven feet tall, wearing blue jeans, black belt and brown loafers, and a tight polo neck with the words **DOES IT LOOK LIKE I GIVE A SHIT?** printed across the front in black. Mike approaches him, fearless, and taps him on the shoulder. The doormen crowd round this guy, who sips a pint of lager, eyes moving from side to side. He and Mike exchange pleasantries. He puts his pint down and has a line of froth on his upper lip. Then he makes a break for it.

It takes all four of them to get the guy down. Getting him out of the club is another matter, and, for a long time, the struggle to the door looks beyond them. After half an hour, I'm almost at the point of going upstairs to ring Abasi who works at a bar down the road until midnight, but finally, they get this guy over to the fire exit. He's on all fours at the bottom of the steps like a dog, his arse pointing back into the club. Pete Bone and Rick have his front, Rick trying to manoeuvre him into a sleeper, Mike and Pete 2 have his legs, slowly sliding him up the steps. He tries to grab onto the stone but it's wet and grimy.

"Can you smell that?" says Rick.

"What?" says Pete 2.

"What are you on about, Rick?" says Pete Bone.

"Come on," says Mike, "let's just get him out."

I sniff the air—it's unmistakable.

It's then that I see a brown stain slowly flowering around his arse. It gets bigger and bigger as they lever him up the stairs, an inch at a time.

"What the fuck is that smell?" pants Pete Bone.

"Why can I smell shit?" says Rick.

"Yeah, he's shit himself," says Pete 2.

Eventually, they get the guy out and he lies on his back on the pavement in the rain. The doormen stand over him and we all know he's not getting up. His t-shirt is ripped and in shreds.

"I bet he gives a shit now," says Mike.

Pete Bone spits blood from a split lip and wipes his face.

*

I used to have a conscience.

*

On my week off, I do nothing for the first few days but lie in, indulging in that sordid luxury that is called smoking in bed. I watch episodes of *Boardwalk Empire* and *Dexter*, and drink endless cups of tea—in the evenings, I spice things up a bit by adding a dash of some awful whiskey Harrison got me last Christmas. When it comes to eating, I order takeaways. I haven't used my kitchen to cook, ever. On Wednesday, I decide to go to the supermarket where I discover Jack Daniel's and Coke in a can and I buy a crate and drink three on the way home. On Thursday, I break and go to The Bellhop for a pint and, inevitably, spend the rest of the week there, with the other reprobates who have nowhere else to go.

*

On the Friday or the Saturday, I see Chuchy walking towards The Bellhop. I'm sitting outside smoking with Luke the barman who has slept with all the girls and whose Movember moustache is now a permanent look. He's also the only person I've ever met who applied for a job at McDonald's and had his application rejected. We're talking about history. Chuchy walks up to us.

"Alright, Chuch?"

"How's it going?"

"Chuchy," I say, "where did you get that hoody?"

"This one?" It's grey and faded and I'm pretty sure it's been in the cloakroom for the past 6 months. "Munks' cloakroom."

"I knew it—you pikey bastard."

"Does your mother not buy you any new clothes?"

"Easy, boys, I came to town without a coat last night and I got cold."

*

A week later, I see him wearing a Nike jacket that's been in the cloakroom for a month. The week after that he's wearing a Topman cardigan that's only been there a few days, and, upon closer inspection, a red and white stripy scarf that some guy left in there last night.

*

One day, something magical happens. Fuming Willy starts smiling. His change of public demeanour and sudden drop of surliness and general grumpiness, coincide with him splitting up with his girlfriend. When I ask Freddy Nelson about it, he frowns, a dark look on his face, and mutters something about her cheating on him a shit load of times, taking loads of drugs, going off the rails, overdosing, and a whole load of other stuff.

A week later, Fuming Willy tells a joke. A week after that, he runs onto the dance floor and joins Dancing Man in jumping around to 'Disco Inferno' during the first ten minutes of Cheese Night. And then I know—even though you can never fully understand transformations like this, losing the girl isn't always a bad thing.

*

Alone in the club, in my office after a reckless dubstep night, when there are always lots of complications with the till split, lots of people to pay and lots of boxes to fill on the cash sheet. Apart from the ubiquitous and relentless music, I like these nights—they keep me on my toes and I get a kick when everything runs smoothly. But they drain you—sometimes I don't leave till the sun comes up.

I look at the time on the computer screen—06:06.

Beer? No—it will put me to sleep.

I get up to go and get a can of Coke from the office and the next thing I know I'm lying on the floor. My clothes wet through with sweat. No breath at all. Shaking.

I get up and look at the time on the computer screen. 11:07.

*

Meet Mitch, Munks' emaciated photographer. He comes and goes with his camera around his neck, anorexic girlfriend hanging from his arm. His current function is taking pictures that make the club look a lot busier than it is or has been for a long time. Dom found him from only God knows where, and I'm not entirely sure of the arrangement they have—sometimes Mitch turns up, sometimes he doesn't. I have no idea if he has another job although I'm inclined to say he doesn't, as he always comes to the bar at the beginning of the night, counts out £2.50 in 5ps, 10ps, and coppers, moaning that this is the only pint he can afford. Then, towards the end of the night, he hunts me down and bothers me—eyes glazed, gurning, ill-nourished, somehow drunk even though he has no money—waiting to get paid, his anorexic but not terribly unattractive girlfriend standing a yard behind him and looking at the floor.

"Are you eating properly, Mitch?" I ask him.

He shrugs, "We don't get hungry often."

I hold out his £20 and give him a pen to sign the receipt.

He signs, smiles, takes his money and leaves.

I go to take the upstairs bar till next and Bran is there with a few of his dubstep-loving, proper gangsta white boys and they are drunk—Bran leaning over and asking Blizzie to do three Jägerbombs and giving her 50p. I recall a conversation I had with him yesterday about him not having any money, and I go behind the bar and take the till which is overflowing and I think how easy it is to get drunk for free in a place like this.

*

Another Cheese Night down and somehow, both down-stairs tills are forty quid up. I go out into the club for answers—Freddy Nelson, Bran, Vickie and Fuming Willy are drinking beer and smoking.

"Erm, guys," I look at Willy and Vickie, "why are the tills up by so much?"

"Oh, because of the 5p increase on house spirits," says Vickie.

"Yeah," says Fuming Willy, "you haven't changed the prices on the tills."

"Well, it's good to know that some people can still add up," I say. "Freddy, Bran—you both owe me forty quid for not charging the new prices."

"What?"

"I'm joking, don't worry. But you two can learn some-thing from the Fume and Smiler."

"The Fume!" shouts Bran, and gives his high-pitched little giggle.

"I sound like a superhero."

"Maybe you are, Willy, maybe you are. Now, go to the cellar and get me a beer."

I go back to the office, open up Internet Explorer and struggle to believe my eyes when I see that yet more Google searches have appeared—

how to tan quickly
alcoholism is not sin it's a brain chemistry disease
i don't earn enough to get a mortgage

*

Next door, sometime on a Sunday with the Fume, Bran, and Freddy Maytal, feeling like dirt, feeling like the damned, drinking cider bombs and pints of Guinness with no concept of time—I've left my wallet at home and have to start a tab.

Behind the bar, Cub and Nick, the other assistant manager who lives on a barge and has just had twins, are turning the place into a scrapbook—cutting up a month's worth of newspapers and magazines and sticking pieces to the back wall where the optics and other bottles are.

I turn to Freddy and ask him if he's trying to get a mortgage. He looks at me like I've just asked him to go to bed with me.

*

When I go in to pay my tab the next day, it seems I have no concept of money either.

*

Meet the middle-aged couple sitting on the sofa downstairs. They are regulars and tonight, they've had far too much to drink and are consuming each other's faces. I stand under the arch by the fire exit and the bar, watching his hand under the table as it gets closer and closer to disappearing up her skirt. Then it does, and stays up there for several minutes. I see her shuffle, a smile on her face as a pair of white knickers slide down her bare legs onto the floor.

Right, this has gone far beyond heavy petting.

I walk over to their table, making a point of picking up the empty cups, and say, "Alright" and stare at them for a couple of seconds—into faces completely devoid of guilt.

When I've taken the cups to the bin and resumed my stakeout position, I see her lean down, grab her knickers and put them in her handbag.

He takes her hand and they go to the almost empty dance floor and Aaron puts on 'When You Were Young' by the Killers and although I believe in coincidences, this is too much of one, and I look up at the DJ booth to see him smiling. He gives me a thumbs up and we watch the middle-aged couple dance.

*

It's early, but not yet light as I walk home, and when I'm no more than twenty yards from my flat door, I see the middle-aged couple again—on the corner of the opposite street. She has her back against a lamppost, and he's lifted her up off the ground. His face is buried in her neck, trousers around his ankles, belt buckle jangling. I stand there for several seconds, dumbfounded. Her eyes are shut. Then she opens them and looks directly at me with clouded pupils.

I shake my head as if to say—*what the fuck are you doing?*

And then I realise they're not going to stop. She shuts her eyes again.

There is absolutely no shame after 4 am.

*

I'm woken up in the morning by my phone vibrating on my face. I roll over, find it and look at the screen—*Chuchy calling…*

I answer it and hold it to my ear.

"What do you want, Chuchy?"

Nothing. A voice in the background. Static. His fucking pocket.

I turn it off and go back to sleep.

*

The Fume and I are standing by the open fire exit, watching Mike and Sam try to throw out the Milkybar Kid because he's fallen asleep in the corner. It's taking them a rather long time, considering the half-pint size of this chap. He's putting up one hell of a fight—Mike seems to be struggling, his face is red, great drips of sweat on his brow. In fact, it looks like the Milkybar Kid is lifting Mike off the floor. Then I realise why—Sam has got hold of Mike's legs by mistake.

"Sam, you twat, that's my leg!"

Eventually, they get the kid out and shut the fire doors. Mike leans on his knees, catching his breath, Sam scratches his neck, his big ears crimson, his gelled hair still perfect, face as gormless as usual. Then Mike stands, reaches up and slaps Sam round the head.

*

Early on a Cheese Night and two scantily dressed drunk girls wearing bunny ears come up to the door till and say, "It's raining on the dance floor."

"Yeah, yeah," says Mike, "and it'll start snowing at 1 o'clock."

But when two more people say the same thing on their way outside for a smoke, one of them Dancing Man ("The dance floor is really wet and slippery!"), we decide to go and investigate. Mike and I push our way through the crowd of pissed students doing the Macarena, over to just in front of the DJ booth, an area which people are giving a wide berth because water is pissing down from the ceiling.

Mike goes straight over to Clive, gesturing for him to cut the music off and a few seconds later, the place is plunged into silence, the lights come on, Mike is on his radio and the other doormen appear—Pete 2 stands at my shoulder looking up at the water coming down and says he'll ring one of his plumber mates then disappears. Meanwhile, the fire doors are opened and the bouncers start evacuating people from the building—there is a lot of discontentment, people asking for their money back, and Mike has to shout, "If you don't get out there's a chance you could be electrocuted," and I'm left standing alone below the burst pipe, only vaguely aware that I'm soaking wet and it's barely midnight.

*

We're sitting around the usual table, feeling strange because we're sipping beer and it's only just 1 am. Pete 2 and his plumber mate Alf are still over by the DJ booth trying to sort out the burst pipe.

I light a cigarette, look around at them all and say, "Right, come on—own up, who keeps using my computer to look up ridiculous things on Google?"

They stare back at me blankly. I direct my gaze at Freddy Maytal and Bret.

"Which one of you was interested in John Travolta's six year gay affair?"

Laughter. I send Little Harry to the cellar for more beer.

Then the Fume says, "It's probably Dom, to be honest."

"What a faggot," says Bran.

"Look, guys, leave him alone," says Freddy Nelson. "He's a nice chap."

"Really, Nelson?" says Tattoo Paul.

"Yeah, he's a legend."

"Fuck off," says the Fume, "he's an arsehole."

"He's not; I've spent like the last two weeks with him every day—you guys haven't really gotten to know him like I have."

Nelson has been helping Dom in his 'promoter duties' recently. Unpaid, of course. Nelson just likes his music and he does media communications at uni—whatever that entails.

Tattoo Paul puts his fag out in the cup in the centre of the table. "Thing is, Nelson would say Harold Shipman was a nice guy if he spent too much time in the same room as him."

"Naked," says Bran.

"Georgie says Dom has a huge cock," says Tanya. "Is that true, Nelson?"

Nelson shakes his head, finishes his beer, says, "Fuck off you lot," grabs his car keys off the table and says he's going home.

*

Acoustic Array night. I'm in my office doing the rota late because I got too drunk yesterday, when Dom comes in. He stands in the doorway and says, "Erm…"

"What?"

"Erm… tonight, for the bands, if you can get away with it—don't give them any of the cans of Carling in the cellar."

"Are they expecting any?"

"Well, yes… but don't give it to them, even if they ask."

"Why?"

"Erm… just don't."

"But isn't that Carling expressly there for bands to drink?"

"Well, yes…"

He wheedles away without saying a word more. I have a horrible taste in my mouth and booze and fags are not entirely to blame.

Later, I make an effort to give the bands all the extra beer they want.

*

I struggle to keep up with the love lives of my staff. Bran and Blizzie were sleeping together, but that's over now and Blizzie is seeing one of Nelson and the Fume's housemates called Handsome Pete, but Blizzie and Nelson also slept together last weekend according to Facebook (Georgie puts a picture up of them wrapped around each other under a duvet on a sofa somewhere). Inez (who has come back to do a few shifts) and Tattoo Paul are seeing each other, the Fume and Cub apparently have a thing and I think Little Harry is gay, although I saw him getting off with a girl last week in the upstairs bar on his night off.

*

Sitting around after a quiet Saturday, Jordi Bone has his Mac out and is playing funky music, and we're all drinking beer and talking about the idiots that came through the doors when Gately pipes up with, "My girlfriend's pregnant."

After the usual, "Congratulations" and "Wows" and "How many weeks?", I look up and have to hold my tongue when the words—why are you keeping this child?—come to my lips.

*

Meet Haddock Pants, a name that has become attached to her only recently but one that has become so affiliated with her that nobody can remember what her real name is. She's the sort of girl that could be attractive but makes herself unattainable by dousing herself with too many layers of vulgar makeup. And when you also realise that she wears the same pair of shiny leggings every time she goes out, you begin to wonder how often she washes them, and just how bad they smell.

*

Nelson comes up to me at the end of one Empire night and tells me that a hot girl just kissed him whilst he was collecting cups. I ask him who and he describes a dark beauty with alluring eyes.

*

A week later, I see Haddock Pants flirting with him at the bar and he comes up to me a few minutes later and tells me that was the girl and I can only laugh and say, "Not Haddock Pants?" but he doesn't hear me because the music's too loud.

*

Chuchy is DJing upstairs and Mike has to keep going over with the sound level gauge because Chuchy keeps turning up the volume and the room is packed because, for some reason, everybody is up here and downstairs is empty. 'You Can Do I' by Ice Cube is playing and people are falling over pissed, there are puddles everywhere and no room to mop them up. Bret and the Fume are sweating behind the bar, and I fight my way through to them and see some guys are doing drugs in the corner—one of them leans down with a note to his nostril and I stand above him and tap him on the head as his snout descends. He looks up and gives me a guilty smile, and I gesture towards the fire exit in the corner before blowing his powder off the table like I'm blowing my birthday candles out, which is when he stands up and pushes me but I've already called Stacie on the radio and he comes over, and, at the sight of his huge arms, the guy flees through the door that I'm holding open. And when the tide parts, I look through to see Nelson, absolutely fucked, draped around Haddock Pants, his face blotchy which means he's been drinking Murphy's, his hair dank, mouth covered in lipstick which is continuously being reapplied courtesy of Haddock Pants who is out of her head and keeps falling asleep, but Nelson is determined to take her home, even when Paul and I slap him awake and try and convince him to go with Paul to the cloakroom to sober up. Then I close the doors, and have the drunks all thrown out, Nelson and Haddock

Pants among them, only for Nelson to ring the club phone ten minutes later and ask to be let back in. He stumbles through the door, fights every wall on his way down the stairs, and all he wants to know when he gets to the bottom is what happened and why he has no money and no drugs left.

*

Sitting in the cloakroom whilst Tanya goes to the Ladies' and then outside for a cigarette—I've put her in here because Tattoo Paul disappears every few weeks to work as a backstage hand at gigs and festivals. Tanya has used masking tape to make the words **TANYA LOVES PAUL** below the hatch, and I'm wondering why the hell there is a really, really, really bad portrait (think kid let loose with vibrant coloured paint) on a canvas, leaning against the wall, on top of all the other crap that's kept in here.

'Heart of Glass' by Blondie comes on and I think of Harrison, who used to sing along to this song, and I see his name written on the walls—

HARRISON HAS HAIR LIKE PAT BUTCHER

And on another wall—

**HARRISON FANCIES ROSIE
FROM NEIGHBOURS**

He's currently touring the states with his band and I'm happy for him, glad that one of us got out of here, that one of us has escaped.

I HATE MUNKS AND GANGRAPE
IT CAN AND WILL GO WRONG

You could sit in here forever and read the graffiti, disappearing entirely without realising a thing. I lean back and look at the ceiling.

WHY THE FUCK ARE YOU
READING THE CEILING?

*

The last Saturday of the month means Dave Abbott's famous Brooklyn—he has Harry D in until midnight with his usual snapback cap and round glasses, bobbing his head, drinking Bombay and tonic, playing funky house music to a lively crowd waiting for the headliners to come on—you may have heard of them, they're called Groove Armada. There is constant traffic through the door and I'm running around trying to deal with everything—the fight by the cloakroom, the sick on the stairs, the prick at the bar demanding his money back because the energy drink we serve isn't Red Bull (I even put big signs up behind the bars last week exclaiming: **OUR ENERGY DRINK IS NOT RED BULL, BUT IT STILL GIVES**

YOU WINGS!)—and I sit down on a stool by the door till for a breather, rolling a cigarette and wondering why Vickie and all the bouncers are pissing themselves, and I look at Mike for answers, whose whole head has turned scarlet, and he's bent over with his hands on his knees, coughing, and he manages to point at Pete Bone, who is standing by the doors, regulating the flow of customers coming in and out, and I see that somebody has stuck an A4 sheet of paper saying **SORRY, OUT OF ORDER**, on his back, and I join in the laughter and spill my tobacco everywhere, and Pete Bone keeps turning around and saying—"What?"

*

Café (that is no longer a café), early evening. I have candles on the tables to create a bit of atmosphere and there are a few people in—DJ Tim setting up for later, Little Harry and The Fume having a pint at the bar. Two lads in snapback caps walk in, bleary-eyed, stoned.

They come up to the bar.

"Erm, do you sell wine?" asks the one wearing a Chelsea shirt and a grey hoody.

"How much do you want?"

"Erm," Chelsea looks at his mate, who shrugs. "Three bottles. Is it alright to take away, yeah?"

"Yeah, of course, mate."

We've been trying to shift crates of the stuff for months —Terry ordered it in ages ago when he and Karen decided the people they wanted through the doors drank cheap, shit red wine.

It takes me a while to find the bottles in the cellar and dust them off. I take them upstairs and give them to the lads, whose eyes light up.

"How much, mate?"

"Thirty-five quid."

"No problem, mate."

They reach for their wallets and put the money on the bar.

"Wait," I say. "I have a proposition for you guys."

"What?"

The Fume and Little Harry Pimm's are back at the bar, looking on with interest.

I get a bottle of black vodka from the spirit shelf, a wine glass, and a straw. I turn the wine glass upside down, put it on the bar, unscrew the bottle, and pour a little black vodka onto the base. I hand Chelsea the straw.

"If one of you can snort that off there, and walk out of here without puking, you can have the wine for free."

He looks at the straw. "Seriously?"

I hold out a hand, "Seriously."

Chelsea takes the straw, "Fuck man, who could turn down a chance like this?"

"Good man."

He puts the straw up to his nose and leans down. The straw end teeters over the oily liquid. Submerges. He snorts.

"Oh, man!"

Chelsea boy steps back holding his nose, black vodka leaking from his eyes. Half the liquid is gone. He hands the straw to his mate, who steps forward and snorts the rest up.

They stumble around the bar, clutching their faces, saying, "Man... man... it hurts... Why did we do that?" and the Fume and Little Harry Pimm's are shaking their heads at them, and I smile and take their money and put it in the till.

"Hang on, mate, hang on. You said if we did it, we could have the wine for free?"

"I said if *one* of you could do it. I'm afraid you did half each." I hold my hands up, saying, "That was the deal."

"Aw, man. You did us."

They take their wine and walk out the door, grumbling and crying black tears.

*

Meet the dude in a black bandana, sitting down at the round tables in the upstairs bar, head leaning back against the wall, asleep with his mouth gaping open. I look at Mike and we both approach him. We stand right in front of the table for a few seconds and then we both see the blonde head in his lap. It's nodding up and down.

Ten seconds pass. Bandana man is oblivious to us standing there—eyes still shut. He makes a horrible noise. Then Mike knocks on the table. She jumps up, bangs her head. His eyes fly open, mouth shuts. They stare at us—sober enough to be horrified, drunk enough not to cry. Her face is bright red. Mike says, "I think it's time for you two to leave," and they get up and are out of the place in seconds.

"Christ, she was a real minger," says Mike.

"Well, it's not like you get classy birds doing that, is it?"

*

We see her a few weeks later with a different bloke. Mike gives her a wink as she comes in and her face goes red again.

*

Around the table after the night has ended and Freddy Nelson is making a list on the notes application on his iPhone entitled **GIRLS BEDDED**. It's a long list and we are all disgusted.

*

Friday, early evening, only the café bar is open. It's getting warmer outside, Bret and Bran are working, Callie is propping up the bar drinking half shandies, and I'm sitting drinking a triple espresso with a large brandy in it to chase away yesterday's hangover. Vickie and Freddy Maytal have the night off because it's his birthday and they have popped in for a few here before heading on elsewhere. Bret has put 'Bad Boys' by Bob Marley on Spotify and we're singing along, changing the lyrics so it goes like this:

Bad Fred, bad Fred, what you gonna do
What you gonna do when he comes for you?
Bad Fred, bad Fred, what you gonna do
What you gonna do when he comes for you?

Freddy is doing an excited little dance and I tell Bran to pour out six shots of Tuaca and we toast Freddy's birthday and tip them back.

*

I meet Harrison for a pint a few hours after he arrives back from touring the states.

"How was the road then, rock star?"

"Long," he says. "How's Munks?"

"Still there," I say, "for the moment."

"Terry still got *big plans* for it?"

"Don't start. He still says he wants to open the kitchen again soon, when summer comes around again, when there's nobody in the city apart from the people who will never leave it."

*

Summer is almost here again and the students are going home, some of my staff among them. Daniel wants assurance that he'll have a job to come back to in September but I avoid giving him an answer as I have no intention of re-employing him—he's started to get on my nerves.

Freddy Maytal informs me that he and Vickie are looking for flats in Brighton so their departure is imminent, but I still have Freddy Nelson, the Fume, Bret, Gately, Georgie, Blizzie, Paul, Tanya and Bran all staying in the city for the foreseeable future and wanting steady shifts. I also take on DJ Euro Pigeon's girlfriend Kerry, who used to manage a club down the road which has just shut down. With the grand reopening of the café on the horizon, I hastily put her in charge of running it. I get CVs through the door most days but the majority of them go in the bin after we've had a good read, playing find the typo and wondering why people always want to work here.

*

Terry finally reveals his plans to me for re-launching the café. I'd only come up to his office to tell him we need a new ice machine.

"Tapas," he says.

"You want to serve tapas?"

"I think it could work."

"But next door serves tapas."

"We're going to serve better."

"And who is going to cook this tapas?"

"Maria."

"The new cleaner?"

"I have it on good authority that she is a fantastic cook."

"Whose?"

"Just trust me."

Because that worked before, Terry.

"When do you want to open?"

"Dom and I are working out the details. Soon."

It's only when I'm back downstairs, walking through the mess still to be cleaned up (the new cleaner likes to do it in the afternoons), the cups, the vomit, the puddles, the piss, the place reeking post Cheese Night, that I remember why I went upstairs in the first place. I go to the old ice machine by the cellar door. It's one of two that Ian bought years and years ago and it's been here longer than any employee. The other is next door in The Bellhop and has been looked after much better than this one. I grab a broom and give the machine a wallop until the ice inside rumbles and falls down.

*

One morning, I receive the best CV you will ever read:

NAME: Clark Eduard Kent
DOB: 1.4.87
4 A levels: History (A), Politics (A), Geography (A), French (A)
University of Edinburgh 2009 – present (reading History and Politics)

EMPLOYMENT:

Bar staff/waiter at Thames Narrowboats
January 2008 – March 2008

- Learnt basic skills in drinks preparation/serving/ bar management
- Role of entertainer too
- Once saved a woman on a hen night from (almost) certain death by drowning
- Knowledge of basic mechanics required due to doubtful seaworthiness of boat

Sales Assistant at Big Dipper Toy Shop
June 2008 – June 2008

- Senior staff member in charge of Skates section with a daily turnover above £10,000 when busy
- As a consequence of demonstrator duties, can now fire juggle, twirl clubs, skate (boards, shoes), perform magic tricks, etc.

Barista at Big Momma's Italian Café
August 2009 – October 2009

- Learnt to make coffee. And tea
- Became very good at cleaning floors, toilets etc. and obeying orders without question or hesitation

Bar Staff at Edinburgh Uni SU
November 2010 – present

- Learnt much more about drinks preparation/ serving. Am now awesome at it
- Went to a course on cocktail making so got that covered as well. Largely

- Acquired knowledge regarding licensing laws, etc., as well as how to change barrels
- Further honed my already esteemed customer relation skills and "Banter"

Miscellaneous Information
- I am tall, 6 ft 3, perfect for those high shelves!
- Punctual and very rarely sick
- Reasonably coordinated
- Fearless. Will keep the peace, no matter the danger
- Fluent French speaker, conversational Spanish
- Able to work from 13th June to 10th September

*

I give him a call and ask him in for an interview.

*

"So, tell me about your time on Thames Narrowboats."

"Erm… it was good."

He is tall (his CV doesn't lie about that) and he wears smart polished shoes, jacket, tie, with his shirt tucked in. His hair is combed back like Clark Kent and I keep expecting him to rip off his shirt and have a Superman vest underneath. I really hope he does.

"Tell me about how you saved this woman from drowning."

"Erm… she fell in."

"Right. You didn't push her then?"

"No."

"Well, that's good."

"Yeah, and well, she flapped around in the water and stuff and I just jumped in and got her."

"Quite the hero," I say.

"Yeah."

"Some might even say, a superhero."

"Well, I wouldn't say that. Anyone would have done it."

"I'm sure they would."

I look at him until my smile drops, and then back down at his CV.

"So, Clark—you can juggle?"

"I can indeed."

"I bet that's handy."

"Yeah."

I look back down.

"And you were a senior member of staff at Big Dipper Toy Shop… although you were only there for less than a month?"

"What?"

"Your CV says you started June 2008, and left in June 2008…"

"Oh." His face is red—his slicked-back hair doesn't look nearly as impressive as it did when he cruised in here with brass balls. "Typo. It should be July."

"Right."

He wipes his brow. "Sorry."

"No need to apologise, these things happen in life. But it's always best to go through your CV carefully before you put it through the door of a potential employer."

He gives a meek smile.

"So, from Big Dipper, you moved onto Big Momma's Italian Café… where you learnt to make coffee. And tea."

"Yep."

"Good skills to have, handy in a café too. And you are brilliant at obeying orders without question or hesitation… I wish I had more staff who could do that. Just last night, I told one of my employees to unblock a toilet and they wouldn't do it. Can you believe that?"

He shakes his head then begins to nod—"You can rely on me."

"I'm sure I can."

I look back down.

"So, you have plenty of bar experience?"

"Lots."

"Wonderful. Cocktails too."

"Yep."

"So, if I asked you to make me a Bullshitter you would have no problem doing that?"

He scratches his head and diverts his eyes. "I've never heard of that one."

"Really? I'm surprised. Lots of people drink it around here."

"I'll have to try it."

"You will."

I look back to the table.

"And you have excellent customer relation skills and 'banter'…"

He says nothing.

"I'm sorry, Clark, but somehow I'm not sure I believe that, and I'm just going on what I've seen in this interview."

I make a point of writing down on his CV in huge letters so he can read it upside down—**RUBBISH AT 'BANTER'!!!**

"But you are rarely sick, I see…"

"Yes." He speaks quietly now.

"Perfect. But only reasonably coordinated? Do you fall over often?"

He says nothing. Fiddles with something below the table.

"Tombez-vous souvent plus?"

He doesn't look up.

"¿Se queda más a menudo?"

It's at this point that he can't stand the game anymore and stands up. I stand too and hold out a hand—official, brisk, straight-faced.

"I need someone fearless. It's a fundamental characteristic in a toilet valet. You're hired."

He looks down at my hand, turns, and walks out the door.

*

I'm upstairs in Terry's office using the printer when I see the paperwork on his desk that tells me he's just signed a new lease with Ian for the building, but under another company name—what was MUNKS LIVE MUSIC VENUE LTD has become MUNKS LTD.

And he thinks tapas is the answer?

*

Next door on a quiet Sunday evening, listening to the Velvet Underground's *Loaded*—'Oh! Sweet Nuthin" is playing and I'm sitting at the bar alone, watching a group of reprobates as they do the Centurion—a shot of beer every minute for one hundred minutes—because they're bored. They're on seventy-five and all have bloated stomachs and are forcing the shots down, egging each other on. I order a large Havana Club on the rocks which I pay Cub twelve pence for and sip it as 'New Age' comes on, and I look at the stand of small booklets displayed by the pumps—**A GUIDE TO SMARTER DRINKING—CONTROL YOUR UNITS**—and I pick one up and read it, but can't take in any of the words, because all I'm thinking about, as the reprobates do their hundredth shot and one of them is sick on the table, is how with each generation comes a new pathway to decadence.

*

The sad thing about it is that Maria's tapas is particularly good. There's just nobody in to eat it except for the staff. Kerry puts a lot of effort into getting the café up and running again. She even persuades Terry to get a box of Pimm's in for the Queen's Diamond Jubilee. I feel sorry for her when I find the box a month later at the back of the cellar, one bottle missing and still sealed behind the upstairs bar.

*

One of my more artistic members of staff has drawn a picture and stuck it up on the downstairs bar noticeboard, next to my **THANK YOU FOR YOUR HEARING-RELATED COOPERATION** and **THANK YOU FOR MOPPING UP THE PUDDLES** notices. It is a biro drawing of a rather macabre and ghoulish man with thick scars and razor stubble—a man who has done a lot of time, who knows where absolutely all of the bodies are buried. And underneath it, the artist has scrawled—

WHAT PEOPLE THINK
THE OWNER OF MUNKS LOOKS LIKE

*

A week later, somebody has added another picture below it—a comical kid's drawing of a bald-headed little man jumping up and down with his arms in the air. Written underneath is—

WHAT THE OWNER OF MUNKS
REALLY LOOKS LIKE

*

I find it too hilarious to take down. A week later, we all start calling Terry T-WAT.

*

Early evening, it's about to turn dark and I'm in the café with Kerry. There's a teenage girl called Little Blue Wolf in playing acoustic guitar and singing—she plays chilled tunes and she's pretty good. Her grey-haired father sits at the table nearest her wearing the smart jacket of a younger man. He's been here since she came in to set up two hours ago, been drinking the same pint of cider shandy the whole time. Next to him is a younger guy wearing a dapper suit and red shoes, drinking a glass of red wine from one of the dusty bottle. The two of them don't seem to say very much but what they do say always makes them both laugh.

The atmosphere is good tonight—there are quite a few drinkers around the tables which Kerry has livened up with candles stuck into glass bottles. We watch a guy at the bar with fuzzy afro hair, who looks a bit like Ralph from the Muppets, painstakingly roll a cigarette until it is perfect. His hands shake. His eyes are hooded. He is fucked. He puts the finished article in his mouth, looks down at the candle in the Jack Daniel's bottle, and leans forward to light it. Neither of us has a chance to shout over to him before his hair catches fire. It burns for a few seconds before, casual as you like, he reaches up a hand and pats it out. He gets up and smiles at us as he walks past the bar and out of the door, leaving a small trail of smoke behind him. I hear him ask somebody for a lighter.

Kerry and I look at each other and just shake our heads and laugh. I wave a hand in front of my face and frown.

"It stinks when someone sets their hair on fire."

"You've seen that before?"

I've seen everything before.

"Yeah, it used to happen all the time when you could smoke inside."

*

The bouncers are throwing a guy out for smoking on the dance floor. Mike asked him nicely to leave but he refused, and now he's still not going easily and is putting up a good fight. I watch, wondering how many times I've seen this before, looking around for Mitch and his camera—this would make a funny photo for the archives. The guy, who's about six feet, is in an awkward position by the fire exit downstairs, hands planted on either side of the door frame—Sam is dragging him by the jacket from the front, Pete 2 and Mike pushing him from behind, and finally, the guy relents and he's on all fours in the doorway, and Sam is pulling him up the stairs and somehow the guy's jeans are coming down, along with his boxer shorts, and then his bare arse is exposed to all the world and his cock and balls are flailing everywhere and they've almost got him out and I see Pete 2 draw back a hand and slap the guy on the arse cheek. There's an almighty smack and the guy yelps and tries to grab his jeans to restore some modesty. But they're already outside on the street and people are walking past staring. There's a huge pink hand mark on the guy's right cheek, and the four of us stand outside watching him hobble away down Gin Lane, pulling his jeans up, cupping his arse with one hand.

We're all cracking up.

"Fucking hell, Sam, you dirty bastard," says Pete 2.

"Yeah, Sam," I say, "how unprofessional."

"What did you want to do—suck him off? Have sex with him? We were trying to throw him out!" says Mike.

"It wasn't me, it wasn't me."

"Fuck, can you imagine if he goes to the rozzers and says he's been sexually assaulted by the Munks' door staff?"

*

Next door at some unreasonable time in the morning—I've had the night off and spent it sitting at the bar, always just about to go home, but I've had far too many for the road. The road is drunk and so am I. Now the bar is shut and we're hiding in one of the booths so no one can see us through the windows—Nick, Cub, Bran, Luke, and Jeremy. We're talking about the glory days.

"Do you remember when Doherty played Munks?" asks Nick. He has a beard to rival Harrison's and wears a paisley-patterned shirt with most of the buttons undone so you can see his hairy chest and his long crucifix.

"He was in the studio recording for a month, wasn't he?" asks Luke.

Nick nods—"That was a dark month. He stayed here upstairs."

"I wasn't here," I say, "but I can't remember why."

"You were in Europe," says Bran.

"I was?"

"Yeah—you were with Claire."

"Have you seen her recently?" asks Cub.

I shake my head and drink my rum.

"She was in here last week," says Jeremy. "She asked after you. Sorry, I forgot to say."

I say nothing.

Bran coughs.

I stare into my glass, swill the rum around.

"Well, yeah…" says Bran, "I remember Doherty and Kate Moss going over to the Duck to get some coke off Barry. They stood on the corner, smoking a joint, and Chuchy and I walked past on the way here."

"First night he arrived," says Nick, "Doherty comes up to me and asks if I work here, and I say yeah, and he looks me up and down, says I look like a man he can trust, and gives me this blue plastic picnic hamper."

"What the fuck?" says Luke.

"Yep, and he tells me to go and hide it in the building somewhere."

"What was in it?" I ask.

"I didn't know, and I was too scared to look. But I hid it in the loft of the pub. Throughout the month he was here, every so often, he'd come up to me and ask me to go and get it. Then he'd take it into his room for a few minutes, then bring it back out and ask me to hide it again."

"And you didn't look inside it? Bet it was heroin," says Cub.

"Probably crack," says Luke.

Nick shakes his head, "It wasn't drugs. At the end of the month, he asked for it back and, when I gave it to him, he opened it in front of me and in there were great big bundles of cash. Probably twenty, thirty grand altogether. He gave me a bundle and said thanks."

"What was it for?"

"Paying off journalists and photographers."

"How much was in the bundle he gave you?"

"Enough."

"Enough to buy your boat?"

He puts his fag out and stands up, "Almost. Does anybody want another drink?"

I nod—say nothing. I look up at the opposite wall where a picture hangs in a frame below the lights, and it reads STAY WITH ME—white words on a sky-blue background.

*

Meet my predecessors. I see them all in the mirror when I wake up—the dark circles that won't go away, no matter how hard I scrub my face.

*

I'm sitting in my office, smoking a cigarette, staring at my Facebook page, at the screen that shows Pending Friend Requests, at my mother's name, her new surname, the picture of her smiling with her new husband aboard his yacht, both of them wearing sunglasses, and very little clothing, arms around each other. A family. The request was sent almost a year ago but I still can't bring myself to click 'Accept'.

*

Tuesday afternoon, three guys come up to me when I'm outside the café taking a break from paperwork, having a cigarette and not enjoying it one bit. They've all got spanners and screwdrivers in their hands, thick, heavy-set guys with mono brows and creased foreheads. I vaguely recognise the big one.

"You work here?" he asks.

"I'm the manager."

"Right—we're here for the CDJs."

"What?"

"The CDJs."

"Yeah, I got that part. Why are you taking them?"

"FRM told us to."

"Why?"

"Terry hasn't paid his bills."

"Right—how much does he owe you?"

He tells me and I say, "OK, OK, can you do me a favour and hold off while I just make a phone call?"

"I suppose."

Any other day, I wouldn't give a shit if they took all the sound equipment but tonight is Cheese and Dave has a wife and kids to provide for, so I call Terry and ask him if he knows what the hell is going on—he rambles on about this and that but the bottom line is that he hasn't paid FRM, the company who we rent our equipment from. He signs off by saying not to let the guys with the spanners in and I tell him it might not be that easy but he says he has faith in me.

I go back to the heavies who are milling around smoking and polishing their spanners.

"Right, my boss is sorting it now."

"Oh, alright."

And they leave.

I stand there for a while, wondering why it was that easy. As far as I know, my reputation doesn't precede me.

Then they've gone, and I take a breath, start rolling another cigarette, and look down at the road, thinking about my missed appointment with the doctor this morning.

*

"So, how many suppliers does Terry owe money to?"

I'm giving Dave his split after Cheese.

"No idea—all I know is FRM sent the heavies round this morning to get the CDJs."

"I thought this might happen."

"What have you heard?"

He pockets his money for the night. "Well, let's put it this way—it's not going to be long before FRM won't deal with Munks and Terry directly. They'll only rent their equipment to me."

"So, you've got Terry by the balls."

*

I finish cashing up after all the staff have gone and then liberate a bottle of Havana from the cellar to take home with me, putting twenty quid in the pot by the tills labelled—AFTER HOURS. I lie in bed, listening to 'How to Disappear Completely' by Radiohead over and over and over again, chain-smoking, sipping from the bottle but not really enjoying any of it.

*

The doctor does the same thing each time anyway. Asks the questions, takes my blood pressure, weighs me, signs a bit of paper and says to keep the medication going.

Prograf

Sandimmun

Mycophenolate Mofetil
Just names on a box. Take them from the packet. Hold them in your hand. Wash them down.

*

There are nights, admittedly they are very rare, when everything goes right. There are no fights, no problems, no blocked toilets, no vomit, no missing money or massive cock-ups on the till, and we finish nice and early and sit back, drinking cold beer and I look around and think there are many people in this place who should be elsewhere, making the most of what they're good at.

*

The wastage sheet can make for quite entertaining reading at times:

PRODUCT	REASON	INITIALS
Double JD and Coke	Customer being a dick	AB
2 Guinness	Card said no	BH
5 shots of tequila	BRAN!	BH
10 Grolsch	DJ	HP
3 bottles of Weston's	Juggling	FN
3 x Jager	Cheese Night... whoops ☺	FM
Vodka Coke	Apparently lost wallet	WM

The Reprobates

Ginger Beer	Staff	DB
2 House Rum and Coke	BRAN!	FN
Magners	Twat with no money (BRAN??)	TK
Coors light	Spilt... sorry... xxx	LDP
3 Tuaca	Bran has a drink problem & no money	BH
3 Grolsch	Chuchy had an accident	AB
½ bottle of baileys	GONE OFF!!! ROUGH!	TK
4 shots of Sambuca	Cheeky tarts	HP
3 havanas	DRUNK MANAGER	GP
Whisky Coke	BRAN! (SACK HIM!)	WM

*

The last hour on a Saturday night and I'm watching Bran draw on his little brother's face in permanent marker—he's fallen asleep on the sofa downstairs, a huge wet patch on his jeans that's not piss but beer from Bran's cup—and we're all standing around watching and laughing. Someone pulls Bran's brother's t-shirt up and draws all over his hairless chest—penises, swastikas, the word **GAY**, black scribbles to imitate chest hair. Then Slicer wants to take it a step further and he tries to pull down Bran's little brother's jeans to draw on his cock but Bran says absolutely no way, and slaps his brother awake and carries him out of the fire escape into the street. I follow them out there and he asks me if I can call his mum to ask her to pick them up. They sit on the kerb together, Bran holding a cigarette to his brother's lips so he can smoke, and as I watch them, I realise there must be many things I miss out on being an only child.

*

One day, I see Mike in a suit, walking along the street, fresh from the magistrates' court where he was asked to give evidence against the guy who glassed someone on the dance floor last summer. He doesn't see me—I'm blending into the street—but later he comes into work and we're talking about the incident and it's early, just turning dark—Pete Bone, Mike and I are out on the street when a group of lads come round the corner from The Bellhop, four of them trying and failing to hold one lad back— dark curly hair, tanned skin, white t-shirt, trainers, gold chain around his neck—the guy who Mike gave evidence against today. I remember his name is Jazz, and unfortunately, he is not barred from next door and has a habit of going there with his mates and getting pissed up and then riled up and now he's decided to come over here with the sole intention of fighting Mike.

Mike keeps his calm for over half an hour of Jazz's abuse until he finally breaks loose from his mates and swings at Mike, and then they are at each other, up against the railings. Jazz is kneeing Mike in the side and Mike has his throat, and Jazz's mates are getting involved, and Pete is fighting three of them at once, and I'm standing here, wondering how the fuck this has descended to blows so quickly. We're outnumbered, and I have to duck a punch from one of them with my phone to my ear.

"Erm, good evening, yeah, yes, I need the police, please, a group of yobos are attacking me and my doormen... Yes, of course. I'm calling from Munks."

*

I arrive at the café one afternoon to find Dave Abbott standing outside raving. His eye is twitching more than normal and he can't stand still.

"Fuckers! Absolute fuckers! What do they know about it—they're never here!"

"What's happened?"

"I just had a meeting with Terry and Dom and Dom told me that they're ending RAM."

"Why?"

"Because apparently, and I quote Dom, 'after carefully observing the figures, it is no longer profitable to Munks.'"

"Oh yeah, because his nights always are."

"Exactly."

He crushes his cigarette out in the doorway.

"Well, let's see what happens when the guys from FRM turn up again to take away the equipment that they're only allowed because of me." He looks at me. "Sorry, mate."

I hold up my hands, "Mate, I understand."

*

Benjamin Grose

I'm sitting at the bar next door staring at a framed picture of barman Luke which is hung on the wall—he's sitting on one of the bar stools, dressed in a blue suit with a red tie, head cocked to the left, staring into the distance with a pensive look on his face and puffing on a Sherlock Holmes pipe, one hand reaching inside his jacket, the other resting on his left leg which is propped up on something out of the picture.

Cub stands at the pumps. "What do you think?" she asks.

"Erm, yeah. It's very sophisticated."

"He's got another one that he's giving Desmond as a wedding present."

I laugh and order a drink. By the time she's poured my Guinness, I realise that somebody is standing next to me. It's Jackson, looking a lot healthier, if not altogether happier. His clothing is in worse condition than it used to be when he worked at Munks.

"How you doing, mate?"

"Ah, not bad," he says, "things could be worse. In fact, they could be a hell of a lot worse. I have just come from an audition."

"What for?"

"Macbeth."

"Fantastic. When is it on?"

"Oh, I'm not sure. Four, five months' time."

He's searching his pockets for money. After several minutes, he examines the amount in his hand.

"Hmm, Cub can you do me 98p worth of whiskey."

186

"Of course."

"Make it a double, Cub," I say, and hand her more money.

"Ah, very kind of you my friend," says Jackson.

"No problem. How's the cocktail bar?"

"I don't know," he says. "One is currently back on the dole."

"What happened?"

"I don't really know. It just…"

"Wasn't Munks?"

Cub brings our drinks over. We clink glasses and I look him in the eye—"To Macbeth."

*

Café, early evening about to turn into hard drinking hour. I'm behind the bar and Harrison and Desmond are both in, back in town for a while after their latest tour which was a huge success and sold out in every venue. Harrison wears his usual skinny black jeans, brown derby shoes, denim jacket and beanie hat. Desmond his black trilby hat, a yellow Black Keys t-shirt and smart black dinner jacket—he has just invited me to his wedding in a few weeks' time. I didn't even know he had a girlfriend.

A group of chavs from another city are also in, sitting in the corner, talking loudly, drinking pints of Grolsch. One of them is reading the band names on the wall and mispronouncing them. Another being openly racist, telling a story where the N-word is all too frequent. I can see Desmond is holding himself back, listening, gripping his drink which he sinks quickly and I pour him another one.

"I'll have a word, Des," I say.

"Cheers, man."

I go over. "Good evening, gentlemen. I just wonder, possibly, if it's not too much to ask, if you could possibly refrain from using racist remarks when swapping anecdotes."

"What?"

"Fuck's he talking about?"

"What's he on about antidote?"

"Shut the fuck up, Gary."

I smile.

The one who had been telling the story has said nothing. I look in his eyes and see a nasty piece of work.

"Thank you, gentlemen."

Maybe ten, fifteen minutes pass. They talk about other crap—girls, cars, drink. They make Gary, the thick one, come to the bar for more drinks. He stands next to Desmond, who is telling me about the Texas gig they did to close the tour.

Gary holds his nose, turns to his mates who are laughing, and says, "Ahhh, you were right, Dean, they do fucking smell weird."

Desmond jumps up, knocks his stool over, and says, "What the fuck, man, do you know what you are saying?" Harrison is on his feet too, saying "You guys need to get the fuck out of here," and they're all standing up, fighting faces on. They upturn their table and beer goes all over the floor. Desmond is nose to nose with Dean, exchanging words I can't hear—I can only see lips moving—and Gary's face is white. He holds his hands up, saying, "What? What? What did I do?" Then the rest of them are quietening down, telling Dean they should go because they've just seen Abasi appear at the window and knock with his huge hand—just once—on the glass, then he peers in and growls. I nod at him, and he winks—I texted him a while ago telling him we had a few cocks in and might need a hand. Eventually, they are all outside in the street, but Des is still nose to nose with Dean in the doorway, his trilby hat in his hands, and finally, Dean takes a step back, smiling.

"Fucking nigger," he says.

Desmond swings so quick it's over in a second. Dean is holding his mouth and Des is holding his hand, and Abasi is telling the chavs if they don't start walking, he's gonna kick their fucking heads in, so they scarper. We go back inside, I get the first aid kit, bandage up Desmond's hand after examining the gash across his knuckle and pour him a rum on the rocks.

*

One Saturday night, I'm sitting in my office about to cash up when I decide I'm giving up smoking. I go online and order an electronic cigarette. The latest Google search is— *help find ben*

I go out into the club.

"Who is Ben?"

Little Harry, Bran and the Fume look at me blankly.

"What?"

"Who is looking for Ben?"

"Ben who?"

"Seriously, guys, I'm getting creeped out by whoever it is that keeps going in my office and looking up shit on Google."

"Not that it was me," says the Fume, "but I might know who Ben is."

"Who?"

"I was watching Breakfast this morning when I got in and there was some woman on there who is still looking for her son, called Ben, who was lost years ago."

"How many years ago?"

"I don't know... lots. I think he'd be twenty-three now."

"The question is," says Bran, "when do you stop looking?"

"You don't," I say.

A strange silence ensues, and I go back into the office, and I swear this wasn't there five minutes ago, although it is entirely possible that I just missed it first time, but there is another search line:

children sold for adoption

*

Terry has got around the FRM and Dave Abbott problem by switching to another company, one that obviously has no business links with FRM because the new company are mad enough to rent their equipment to Munks. But it's only a matter of time before Terry fails to pay the new supplier and I have more heavies to deal with.

Dave has been appeased for the moment because, as he put it, at least he still runs the two busiest nights in the place. He's not making the money he once was, but let's face it, none of us are.

*

As soon as my electronic cigarette arrives, I stub out my last fag and give my tobacco and other smoking equipment to Bran. The e-cig comes with cartridges, each of which is supposed to last two days, but that same night I get through five of them—I walk through the club, puffing the thing, the little blue light winking at me. It's not bad, but by the end of the following night, I am out of cartridges completely.

*

"WHAT'S YOUR NAME?"

I'm behind the bar because we're a man down again on a Cheese Night, shoulder to shoulder with the Fume and Bret, looking into the red-rimmed wild eyes of the Dutchman who has asked me this every time he's come to get a drink.

"ANT," I say.

"HI, ANT."

"HI," says Ant.

"MY NAME IS KLAUS, I'M FROM AMSHTER-DAM," he says.

"GREAT. WHY ARE YOU HERE?"

"BECAUSE IT'S WHERE THE PARTY IS, AND KLAUS LIKES PARTIES."

"GREAT. SAME AGAIN?" Ant points at his empty cup.

"YES, SAME AGAIN. HAHA. I LOVE THE BRIT-ISH TURN OF PHRASES!"

Ant gives him another Grolsch and he says, "THANK YOU, ANT," and dances away from the bar like a jack in the box, and as Ant watches him, all Ant can think about is nicotine rolled up in paper.

*

Later, Ant is standing under the arch by the fire doors next to the bar entrance, waiting for Clive to play the last song—he puts on 'New York, New York' by Frank Sinatra and the Dutchman is dancing around on the stretch between the dance floor and the bar where the round tables are.

"START SPREADING THE NEWS!" sings the Dutchman, and he starts pretending to swim. "AMSTER-DAM, AMSTER-DAM…" and he tries to involve a random group of girls in his crazy front crawl, half swing, half waltz, "I WANT TO WAKE UP IN A CITY THAT DOESN'T

SHLEEP… AND FIND THAT I'M NUMBER ONE, TOP OF MY LISHT, HEAD OF THE HEAP, KING OF THE HILL…" he comes back over to Ant and Ant only smiles at him, his arms crossed. "THESE LITTLE TOWN BLUESH… THEY'RE ALL MELTING AWAY…" and Mike turns the lights on, "I'M GOING TO GET ABSHO-LUTELY FUCKED… IN OLD AMSHTERDAM!" and for the grand finale, he skids along the floor with his arms raised.

*

The next morning at nine, I go to Boots and pick up a nicotine inhalator and suck it all the way back up to the top of town to get my head straight. I see Pete Bone on the way back up, walking downtown with his son, or maybe his daughter. It's difficult to tell. He/she doesn't speak, wears baggy clothes, has long hair, an androgynous face, and eyes that stare too much.

*

First Saturday of the month which means it's Brooklyn and Dave has some guy, a mate of his called Erol Alkin, coming down from London to DJ for the last two hours. We've already sold out of tickets and the place is packed, and, because I was hungover this morning, I forgot to do the change run. So, I go next door to see if they have any spare, and end up standing at the bar for too long, lots of new staff being slow with drinks, jangling my keys around, looking up at the board behind the bar which says—

SHOT OF THE WEEK
WILD TURKEY
HUNTER S. THOMPSON'S FAVOURITE
"When the going gets weird, the weird turn pro."

When Luke comes back from wherever he's been, I nod at the board and he pours out two shots. A second later, they're gone and then I wipe my mouth and ask how they're doing for change and if he can spare me any. He shakes his head, "Mate, we're fucked too. Nick forgot to do the change run."

"Him too? Bollocks."

And so, I have to go back to the club to get an old backpack that's been in the cloakroom for months and then take the thousand pounds in cash from the change drawer I was supposed to exchange this morning, and head out into town along the strip of bars and clubs and cocktail joints, the many iniquity dens of Gin Lane, dodging the slappers and the clowns, the hen parties and the stag dos, ducking into places as I go and begging for change.

*

I'm walking through the club holding a can of petrol, while Elton John's 'Rocket Man' plays. It's dark in here but I can see everything. I pour petrol onto the floor, beginning in the cellar and weaving a trail through the place, ending by the front door where I stand and throw the empty can away—down over the railings onto the road which is empty even though it's the middle of the day and nobody is around. I pull out a packet of cigarettes that aren't mine, light one, take a single drag and then flick it into the puddle in the doorway...

*

I wake up, naked, in my kitchen, standing over the cooker holding a lighter. I can smell gas. The hob is on—I reach out a hand to turn it off. Then I search my flat for every lighter, every can of fluid, and every box of matches I can find before putting them in a bin bag and throwing them away.

*

I'm woken up the next morning by my phone vibrating. I look at the screen to see *Chuchy Calling* and I reject the call without bothering to look at the time.

*

When I wake up again, I realise two things. One, that I've missed Desmond's wedding. And two, I'm probably not going to make it to the reception either.

I look at my phone. It's almost half past six in the evening. I have three missed calls from Cub, two from Harrison, and a text from a number not in my phone book, but one that I still can't seem to forget.

Will I be seeing you at Des's party later? C x

*

I spend the night sitting by the door till, waiting for everyone at the party to inevitably migrate towards Munks after the bar shuts at the reception. Part of me wishes I was there. Harrison told me Desmond has put five grand behind the bar, Madsen and Dave Abbott are DJing, and everybody is there—drunk, dancing. I text Bret and he says it's a hell of a party.

I tell him and Callie to enjoy themselves.

Around 1 am, a few people start to trickle in, wearing tousled shirts and suits, ties removed, faces flushed. A few faces I know ask why I wasn't at the party. I smile and say that there are times when we have to work even when we really don't want to. And they ask for stamps on their faces instead of their wrists, then go into the almost empty nightclub, leaving me alone thinking that at least this place has given me a good excuse for many a non-attendance over the years.

*

The band playing is called The Love Kills. It's a Thursday night so there's a moderate crowd in. The drink is flowing and the lead singer is taking off his clothes.

"Do you think he does this at every gig?" Mike asks.

We're standing in the usual place on the steps at the edge of the dance floor. His t-shirt comes our way and girls fight over it like a bouquet at a wedding.

"It is rather sporadic," I say. He has one sock on, half his jeans off, and yet he's still wearing his scarf and pork pie hat as he wails into the microphone. "But it does appear to be his party piece."

He gets right down to his underwear, a pair of musty green boxers which are far too tight for a man of his ilk.

"What happens if he gets a boner on stage?" asks Mike.

*

I'm at the top of the steps which lead down to the dance floor, watching the drunk perverts go to work, sucking on my nicotine inhalator and chewing a mint at the same time when some guy comes up to me and says, "Mate, why are you smoking a tampon?"

I stand there for a further twenty seconds after he goes to the Gents', which is when I think fuck it and go and find Bran, take his tobacco off him and hole myself up in the office.

You try giving up smoking in a place like this.

*

Freddy Nelson comes and tells me that he's moving away— to his girlfriend's parents' house in some town north of here.

I didn't even know he had a girlfriend, but apparently, they met at Glastonbury.

"Well, at least you got your degree in the end," I tell him.

He gives me an unenthusiastic smile.

It's only later when I'm talking to the Fume and Bret after the shift that I find out that Freddy failed third year again.

"Again?" I say. "How did he manage that?"

"Fuck knows," says the Fume. "But his parents and sister have been trying to get hold of him for weeks, asking about his graduation…"

"And he hasn't told them?"

He shakes his head.

*

I've just got back from the cash and carry and there's a bald guy in doing the monthly stock take, spread out on a table upstairs with a notebook and last month's wastage sheets— some dog eared, some ripped, all stained with drink.

"Everything OK?" I ask him.

"Well, I wouldn't say that."

He gives me the paperwork as he leaves. I stand in the doorway, looking at the paperwork when my phone starts ringing. I look at the screen—*Mother Calling*—and press the button to reject the call.

*

"Right, guys, please can you make sure that any spillages, mispours, non-payments, everything goes down on the wastage sheet."

There are a few laughs.

"Yeah, stop juggling bottles of Weston's, Nelson," says Little Harry.

"I'm serious," I say. "Terry is getting on my back."

"How was the stock take?" asks Bran.

"Wank."

"That bad?"

"We're four bottles of vodka down."

*

Apart from Terry getting on my back, I'm not too concerned about the bad stock take—it's not the worst. There was a time, many years ago, when I was just a humble bartender, that almost five grand's worth was missing. Back then, it turned out that one of the managers was letting all his mates in after hours and drinking all the booze. Along with the other manager, I helped bring the story to light when Ian was on the brink of sacking everybody as a last resort. He didn't, the culprit was ousted, and Munks went on.

*

A wet bank holiday Monday and I'm sitting at the door till. Freddy Maytal and Tattoo Paul have organised another ska night but it's not enjoying the success of the first one.

Paul isn't here, but up country somewhere working a gig, which means that all his mates who filled the place last time aren't here either.

It is almost 10 pm, and we have absolutely nobody in. The band are called The Hocus—a young group of lads who, when they first arrived, walked through the club awestruck by the names on the walls. They keep asking Freddy when the people are turning up and I feel for the guy when he tells them that hopefully, soon, there should be some people turning up from downtown. Two or three people trickle through the door, pay the £3, and the band goes on at 11 pm and plays ten or twelve songs to these lucky people who have walked into their own private gig. I stand outside with Stacie and Dave Abbott who has turned up to DJ after the band again, and he says, tentatively, "Maybe I won't charge Freddy full price for DJing tonight," and I look up at him and say, "You're a man with a heart, Dave, you know that, don't you?"

*

I go next door because I'm bored and we're dead and nobody's around anymore because Ian has extended The Bellhop's opening hours to 3 am on Fridays and Saturdays, which means Munks is suffering but does he give a shit? Makes no difference to him if Terry fails. I find a fiver on the floor by the bar and stand there, looking up at the board behind the bar:

SHOT OF THE WEEK
AUCHENTOSHAN
Sweet and 40% delicate
£3.35
... like a honey weasel

Luke comes behind the bar wearing the t-shirt a group of us bought him for his birthday, it reads—**MY NAME IS LUKE, NOW TAKE YOUR PANTS OFF** with a picture of him when he was about twelve in his school uniform above the words. I ask him for two honey weasels and then another two and when I go back next door, down to the office to get started on next week's order, I might as well be floating.

*

Welcome to the drunken hour, the time on a Saturday night when people struggle to exert any sort of control over themselves.

I'm standing in the doorway to the downstairs bar and kitchen, staring at the clock high up on the wall next to a newspaper cutting of Gordon Ramsey. There is an old A4 notice stuck below the clock that reads **DO NOT USE UNTIL FURTHER NOTICE**—the ink is smudged and the corners of the paper are curling. Gordon Ramsey has horns. The clock hands are stuck at 4:20.

Four couples are leaning against the bar eating each other's faces. Bran and Bret point a soda gun at each of them in turn and give them a small dousing until they take their heavy petting elsewhere. I forge myself a path through the club. The floor is slippery everywhere. Chuchy is playing 'Gangnam Style' and people are dancing to it like they have some sort of convulsing disease. A guy is asleep on the steps to the dance floor. Sam stands there shaking him. I pick up a glass of water from a nearby table and hand it to him. He pours it over the guy's head, which wakes him immediately and, with Sam's help, he gets back to his feet—bleary-eyed, face dripping.

Chuchy is now playing 'Give Me Everything' and I have to waltz past a group of people dancing by the cloakroom, wailing the lyrics—"GRAB SOMEONE SEXY TELL 'EM HEY!"

I go into the Gents' toilets to find a group of girls in there.

"IT STINKS IN HERE!" one of them yells in my face as they all run away.

The door shuts behind them and I see that somebody has scrawled **04:20?** on the inside of the door. I do a check of the cubicles and see that the same thing has been written on the inside of those doors too.

*

"Hi, Craig."

A girl is at the door till, paying and getting her stamp from Stacie, looking at me like we know each other. I blink at her. Look. She's wearing a t-shirt with a picture of

Bowie on it. Jeans. Boots. Attractive, in a rock chick sort of way.

All I can do is smile as she goes into the club.

"Craig?" says Tanya. "Who is Craig?"

"Who indeed," I say.

It's only when I'm standing outside later, smoking, that I realise that Bowie Girl is Nevermind Baby Girl and I wish that maybe, once in a while, I could tell the truth to somebody.

*

I found a passport this morning—battered, the gold writing almost completely scratched off, out of date. It belongs to a girl called Henrietta Mary, born 1990 in Oxford. I stare at the picture. I know her—it's Nevermind Baby/Bowie girl. Most of the pages are ripped out but someone has written this on the last one: **WHEN I SAW U 2NIGHT, BABY, I IMAGINED CUTTING YOU UP WITH A HANDSAW WHILST FUCKING U TILL U SCREAMED. CALL ME. 07342 419550.**

Horrified, I stare at it for a long time, sitting in my office and chain-smoking. Then I put it in my deepest drawer.

*

At times, after waking, I am unable to do anything but lie in bed, looking around my room at the things I own, the clothes I wear, the books I've never read, just thinking that there is no room in this room.

*

"Who do I speak to about paternity leave around here," asks Gately. It's late into the lock-in after Empire and I'm struggling to see straight.

"Me," I say, looking up from rolling a cigarette. "And the short answer is—no, you don't get any."

*

Monday 5 pm and I get bombarded with text messages from the staff asking if I've been paid yet and why they haven't. I haven't either so I call up Terry—he rambles on while I'm sitting on the tables outside The Bellhop, smoking and drinking an espresso—finally, he says that everything should be fine by tomorrow morning and it's the bank's fault, not his.

But we know better and when our money still isn't in by Tuesday midday, I get another round of disgruntled texts, another at 5 pm, and then, at 10 pm, a severely pissed-off bunch of staff turn up to work Cheese. Tattoo Paul is particularly miffed and tells me he has just called Terry who has assured him the money should be in his account by Wednesday morning.

"Lying T-WAT," he says. "We all know he's having major cash flow problems. Hasn't paid Ian his rent. I've got a good mind to just take my wages out of his tills."

"Don't do that," I say. "I lost half of the float last week."

"How?"

"Remember the last ska night that made no money?"

"Oh, yeah."

*

I have a mass staff exodus when the light begins to fade from the days and we are on the brink of another winter as early as September. Freddy Maytal and Vickie finally (after a year and a half) move to Brighton, Freddy Nelson moves to his girlfriend's parents' house (Tattoo Paul, the Fume and I have a sweepstake going on how long it will be before he accidentally sleeps with the mum) and Tanya suddenly sends me a text one day saying that next week she's leaving for a while—no reason, just because. I say OK, knowing that in a week, a month, three months, I'll get a text from her asking for shifts again. Because as soon as people flee from this city, all they want to do is come back. And in Munks, there is no such thing as a last shift.

*

Meet the group of students at the upstairs bar commit-ting Tequila suicides. They have trails of salty snot on their cheeks and are crying incessantly. The bar is packed and they are shouting "EDWARD" and "CEDRIC" because there's a guy at the bar who looks like Robert Pattison—

he's ordering a Whisky Coke, oblivious even though he must have heard it all before. One of the students—the youngest-looking lad with a baby face who they call Scrappy—is being bullied by the others into drinking a pint which they have Bret pour five different colours of Sambuca into. Instead of a rainbow, it makes an oily black concoction which the little lad downs while they chant and then brings straight back up onto the bar. I go over and tell his mates to take him outside for some fresh air with a pint of water. Blizzie is mopping up the sick with blue roll, a pained look on her face, holding her nose with her spare hand. I tell her she gets a gold star for doing it.

Later, Mike and I throw the rest of the Tequila Suicide Squad out for extreme drunkenness when two of them start pouring pints over their heads and a third steals Mitch's camera, goes to the toilet and takes pictures of his penis.

*

I come in one morning to find the front door wide open. There's a guy kneeling down in the porch, a toolbox next to him, fiddling with the lock.

"Erm—what's going on?"

"Alright, mate—I'm just changing the locks."

"Why?"

"Guy called Terry asked me."

"How many locks?"

"All of them—well, all the main doors."

"Right. Do you know why?"

"No idea. I got a call this morning from this guy Terry —the owner, right?"

"Yeah."

"—well, he told me to come in first thing, met me here and showed me which locks need changing."

"Is he here?"

"Don't think so. He drove off somewhere."

I'm already ringing Terry's number as we speak but it goes to answerphone. I have no choice but to go in and sit at the tables in the café with a large coffee, ringing and texting Terry every so often to try and find out what the hell is going on. I almost text Dom but decide not to. I put a Spotify playlist on that I made the other day called Hell Hath No Fury, go outside and stand at the railings, smoking endless cigarettes and looking down at the busy road. 'London Calling' by the Clash is the song playing inside when I stub out my tenth cigarette on the wall.

*

Around 3 in the afternoon, I get a text from Terry—*Break in at Dom's house. They took his keys. Changing locks as a precaution.*

*

I take a night off, leave Freddy in charge for his final shift before he and Vickie go to Brighton, and go next door to sit on the same stool downstairs, alone for most of the night, drinking steadily but not tasting it. It's Thursday and it's busy and DJ Tim is on the decks playing his usual funk, and I'm just hiding away in the corner, looking at the date again, the date that always comes round too quickly—September 11th. I'm drinking neat Bell's on the rocks, looking at every face and thinking it's her, thinking it's Henrietta Mary. I see her in the crowd and she's wearing a brown pork pie hat, a denim jacket, a strapless flowery dress, jeans and a white t-shirt, white jeans and a blue top, but every time she comes closer it isn't her, it's someone else, and I carry on drinking and drinking until I can't make out a single face in the room.

*

I'm standing on the dance floor. The tables and stools are piled in the middle, ablaze. All around me, the place burns. Glass explodes from behind the bar. The DJ booth is an inferno. I walk through the club, unharmed, watching the fire spread. A song is playing—'Don't Let Me Be Misunderstood' by the Animals. The toilet doors have fallen to the ground, splintered, crackling with flames. I can just about make out what's written on them in thick black felt tip—04:20?

I get to my office and the door is shut. Locked. Untouched by the fire. Water is spilling out from underneath it.

By the time it reaches my feet, it has turned to blood. And there, stained, ragged, floating in the puddle of dark purple, is Henrietta Mary's passport.

*

Wake up, my office ceiling revolving. Use the back of the office chair to pull myself up and onto it. The computer tells me it's almost midday. My desk is strewn with half-drank bottles of beer, plastic cups full of fag butts, change, notes, aspirin. Struggle to remember if I've taken my pills today, yesterday, or this week even? Look at my phone and see I have three missed calls from my mother. Feel my kidney throb and have to hold onto the desk so I don't faint again.

Vomit into the bin until there is nothing left to come out.

*

Bored on a dead Wednesday, a band nobody has heard of called Bastille are playing to a dozen people and I'm upstairs leaning on the counter, watching Tanya paint her fake nails on the door till again—her last shift before she leaves for wherever it is she's going. She tells me Freddy and Vickie had sex in the band room the other night, on their final shift.

"How?" I ask her.

"What do you mean?"

"Well, it's hardly the most accommodating room in the club. Not like Dom's office."

"What does that mean?"

"I saw Georgie and him going up there on New Year's Eve."

"She never told me that."

"Well, she wasn't sober. And it was New Year's Eve. Whose bed were you in?"

"No one's."

"I don't believe that."

*

Gately's baby son is born and he and his girlfriend name him Alfie. He's a cute little thing. They bring him into the café one Sunday and I hold him. He stares up at me, face devoid of a smile, as if he can tell what sort of person I am.

"He likes you," says Gately's girlfriend, Anna.

He starts crying and I hand him back to his mother.

*

I'm thoroughly pissed off with Bret because he's given up smoking and is managing far better than I did. I'm back to fifty a day and my lungs aren't too happy about it.

*

I've got the Fume doing some duty managing. Bret has become unavailable of late and I can tell he's going to leave sometime in the near future.

I'm getting good at spotting when people can't do this anymore.

But when it comes to myself, I can see nothing but a void.

*

I have a night off and for some reason, I end up in the club, standing at the downstairs bar drinking an endless conveyor belt of Havana Club and Cokes with nobody in particular at 1 am. I only came down at 7 pm to bring the Fume a set of keys, but I ended up going next door for a few, and then, when the clock struck midnight, the natural migration to Munks with the other reprobates was inevitable.

Kyle is playing 'Sex on Fire' by The Kings of Leon. The place is half full. I go to my office to have a smoke, sit in front of the computer and type *symptoms of pyromania* into the Google search bar. The screen becomes too blurry to read after five minutes and I lock up the office and go back out into the bar. Little Harry and Blizzie are in on their night off and I shout "Come and join the Havana Club!" and buy the three of us a double and shots of Tuaca before going into the downstairs kitchen with the intention of going to the cellar to get a staff beer when I slip and fall backwards through the fire exit.

*

I wake up to a load of text messages.

The Fume: *REVVING! I have one drunken manager*
Little Harry: *Cheers for the shots! x*

Bran: *BROWN SEAT!*
Mother: *Can you call me please?? X*

*

The vanishing vodka suddenly stops vanishing when Vickie and Freddy Maytal leave for Brighton. I'd known all along that Vickie liked to help herself after hours, I just didn't care enough to do anything about it. Serves Terry right really, he stopped getting in bottles of staff vodka. He still hasn't learnt that people need a constant supply of booze to be able to stand this job.

*

I sit in my office in the afternoon, trying to do the rota for next week, rolling cigarettes every five minutes, drinking cans of Coke one after the other, and throwing the empties into a corner. I keep clicking onto Facebook and putting her name into the search bar and each time it comes up, the girl whose passport is in my drawer, the girl whose face I can't stop seeing.

*

Mike comes to me in a rage.
  "That fucking prick!"
  "Who?"
  "Chuchy."

"What's he done now?"

"Won't turn the fucking music down. He's a fucking prick—I'm this close to barring him!"

I go downstairs where Chuchy is playing 'Titanium' by David Guetta. I stand in front of the DJ booth and look in to see his head bowed, hoovering up lines of cocaine. Kyle is standing next to him doing the same.

They both come up for air and Chuchy holds the note out to me—"There's one for you."

Kyle is completely fucked—leaning against the back wall, spilling his drink, eyes red. Probably had another argument with his fiancée—they usually end up with him in here bollocksed.

"Chuch, listen to Mike when he tells you to turn it down, mate."

"I did—I have!"

He's still holding the note out. I look at it—at the tiny bits of white powder on the end.

Then I go back upstairs to try to appease Mike.

*

I ban Chuchy at the end of the night because on top of everything else—the drugs, getting too fucked on the job, turning up the music too loud, pissing the bouncers off—the silly fucker got caught smoking a joint in the DJ booth. He says that a girl he knows was smoking it and he wasn't, but whatever happened, I have to ban him for a few months just to calm Mike down.

*

On my next night off, I'm in a Bellhop lock-in at about 4 in the morning. Donald, the old, grizzled, grey-haired manager who leaves all the work to Nick and Cub, is a massive coke head—he has poured at least three or four grams of the stuff onto a table and is trying to organise the marching powder into neat little lines. After a while, he gives up—he's too fucked (probably because the only time you ever see him in the bar is when he's pouring another pint of Foster's for himself), and gives his card to a girl to do it for him. When she's finished, there are six or seven identical lines of cocaine, each about two inches long, in the middle of the table. She rolls up the twenty and takes the first.

There's a knock on the door and Cub goes to open it and it's Bran and the Fume, drinking bottles of Coors that they smuggled out from next door.

Cub goes to the computer behind the bar and puts on a song and I recognise it because it's Harrison's band, and we sing along for a little while and I wonder what makes a good man, then my glass is dry and I get Luke to fill it up again. Donald is trying to make more lines of cocaine, and the room is spinning and I'm going to be sick but I don't because I hate being sick. I grimace and take my rum, once, twice, finish it with the third mouthful. Another song from Harrison's band is playing and I feel strange, more people are knocking on the door, and some other guys appear from upstairs and it's getting later and later, the sun is almost up when I take a bottle of Havana rum from behind the bar, promising to replace it tomorrow.

*

I wake up the next morning, hugging the bottle once more, what's left of it sloshing around. I'm crying a little, and it strikes me, deep, deep down, that Munks nightclub is all I've got, and there's a twenty-pound note in my pocket that isn't mine.

*

Sometime later, I walk down to the club. It's raining but I decide to embrace it and the rainwater is definitely not the worst thing I've drunk in the past 24 hours. I tried to shower away last night but it still lingers. I go in through the café door and stand in front of the bar. It's just turning dark. The chairs are all stacked on the tables. The place smells of disinfectant. I go behind the bar. Remember telling Bret last night to leave the till in because it was a Monday and they took no money. I open it for some reason and see the black plastic interior—all the empty places where the cash should be.

*

Terry and I go through the CCTV.
    "It has to be somebody who knows the place," I say.

"Look—he's holding his face at an angle so the camera can't see him—he knows where they are."

The time on the screen is 15:45. Terry and Dom are sitting upstairs in their office, as usual. Downstairs, a guy dressed in jeans and a grey hoody enters from the door between the upstairs bar and the corridor that leads upstairs to the studio. He looks around, goes behind the bar and opens the till. He knows where the spare key is hidden above the fridge, knows how to turn it so the till comes to life, knows which button to press to open it.

"How much was left in the till?" Terry asks.

"Only the £200 float," I say. "And to be fair, that door between the upstairs bar and the studio corridor is always left open. So don't blame Bret. I told him to leave the till in…"

He shakes his head. "Of course not. I'm more interested in this chap."

The guy so desperate he took all the change too.

We pause the screen on what we can see of his face as he leaves—a grey blur turned to the floor—dark hair, no eyes visible.

*

At times, I like to stand outside, hidden in the shadows, looking up at the lead sky, just listening to the drunken conversations of the smokers.

"Last weekend I went to a foot-washing ceremony in Rutland."

"How do you give a dog permission to start eating?"
"I'm gonna rub shit in all your children's faces."
"Do camels really have toes?"
"Why is alcohol legal?"

*

I sit in the office, late after Empire night, drinking beer slowly and looking at an email from Terry.

I want a list of all managers of this place from the last ten years.

My reply—*But surely even if they had kept a key, all the locks were changed two weeks ago?*

And he came back with—*All apart from the outer studio door.*

I almost email him back asking why but I don't need to. For one, it's no secret he's struggling to make ends meet—it's not cheap changing a dozen locks. And two—the entrance that faces The Bellhop has an inner and an outer door—at least it does at night when I lock the place up. It doesn't during the day when Terry and Dom are upstairs doing whatever it is they do up there—the outer door is locked but they leave the inner door open so they can buzz people in without moving.

I look down at my list. It's long. There are some suspicious names on there. At least two had been to prison, one of them with a history of stealing from the place when Ian was in charge.

I send the list to Terry.

*

"Alright, mate."

"Alright."

A Liverpudlian guy with floppy hair who I think I should know is at the bar ordering drinks.

"What's your name?" he asks.

"Joe."

"Cool. Nice to meet you, Joe."

Joe pours him his beer and he pays.

Half an hour later, Joe is walking through the club when he gestures for him to come over to where he's sitting at one of the tables by the doorway that leads to the toilets and upstairs.

"Do you sniff coke, Joe?"

"No."

"But you're the manager?"

"Yeah. So what?"

"I know you from somewhere."

Joe shrugs, "I drink in the pub next door."

He nods. "Well, if you ever want some powder, let me know. Do you want my number?"

"I don't have a phone."

And Joe goes upstairs.

*

Meet the fat girl wearing a salmon pink dress, collapsed on the sofa downstairs, her arms and legs akimbo. Her mouth is open like she's waiting to be fed. You can see the colour of her knickers, although I don't know why you'd want to look. She's taking up the whole of a sofa, which could comfortably seat four normal-sized people.

Mike and Sam go over to her. She opens her eyes, grins stupidly at them, and doesn't move an inch. I'm standing near enough to hear Mike say, after ten minutes of standing there, staring at her, "Oi! Sit up straight, you lazy cow, or I'll throw you out!"

And later, when we throw everyone out and I go upstairs to shut the doors, I see her again. She looks like a large, pink beached whale, riding the pavement just outside the door, skirt hitched all the way up, shouting, "Somebody fuck me! Somebody fuck me!" and staring through the door, crying.

I poke my head back inside and shout, "Somebody go and tell Sam there's a girl outside asking for him!"

*

When I wake up on my next night off, I'm feeling slightly drunk still, which gives way to a childish, fiendish mood in the late afternoon—so I take all the lost credit cards from a drawer in my office, enlist Bran and the Fume as accomplices, and take the train to the next city. We get there around sunset, walking through the warm approaching dusk like a trio from the graveyard shift. We begin a pub crawl, starting tabs in the names of GEORGE M HILL, CHRISTINA YEOMAN, OSCAR PHILLIP CROSS, and JEREMY JK JONES, and leaving their cards behind after running up a sizable slate of pints, shots, cocktails, and snacks. Once we run out of cards, we take the train home, drunk, celebrating the rare occasion that our wallets are unspoilt. But this doesn't last much longer because we go to The Bellhop to carry on drinking, where we don't need to leave a card to begin a tab—our faces are enough. I lose sight of mine soon after 2 am when Nick brings the hard liquor out—a double shot each of Bacardi 151 finishes the three of us on the long haul. Bran collapses underneath the table, the Fume dashes to the Gents' to bring up the night's vast consumption, and the next thing I know, I'm waking up on the sofa in my flat, Thursday morning showing through the gaps in the curtains, unable to do anything but stare at the ceiling, with no memory of the journey home.

*

Meet the mad genius who works upstairs. Dave Turbet, the studio man. He's been here longer than anyone. He has recorded albums with Elbow, The Corral, The Horrors, Richard Ashcroft, Pete Doherty. You'll see him on occasions, when someone is using the studio, wandering around between Munks and The Bellhop, holding a pint of Guinness, wearing his eternal scuffed brown shoes and paisley shirt with the sleeves rolled up. He lives in a village somewhere on the outskirts of the city and he cycles to work on a pink bicycle which he leaves in a hedge somewhere on the road out.

*

Meet the dead society—it's gathered upstairs in the studio. The club is shut and it's some vague time in the early morning. Bran is asleep on the floor by the door, fucked. A guy who used to be in a big band and is now going solo has been recording in the studio for the last week. He sits next to Dave Turbet who is in his old leather armchair in front of a huge computer screen, playing with the controls, smoking endless cigarettes. A black American woman from Oklahoma in her thirties is chatting to Harrison about New Orleans and jazz. Desmond, Marshall and Madsen, the three members of the infamous Slugs, are standing over by the window, drinking directly from a bottle of port, laughing, and making lines on the windowsill. Madsen is tanned and wearing a German SS hat. He's talking about the old Roland 808 that apparently he's got hidden in his attic, and how he could get half a million quid for it, but he's not that desperate yet. A smartly dressed guy from London called Click who smokes Montecristos is talking to Cub about taking her out on a date in Kensington. A dude called Chase from LA, who wears a purple waistcoat over a white shirt with chinos and cowboy boots, is talking incessantly to me about drugs. Another five or six people are sitting or standing around. There are bottles of rum and vodka on the go, as well as the crate of staff beer I brought up. At intervals, the famous artist going solo takes out a huge bag of cocaine from his inner jacket pocket and passes it to a skinhead who stands in the corners saying nothing—he makes up half a dozen lines on a CD case, then does another, and passes them around the room. One of the CD cases is 'The House That Dirt Built' by the Heavy. The other—'No Exit' by Blondie. I pass when it comes to me. Somebody rolls a joint.

Chase turns to me and says, "What is the worst thing you have ever seen?"

The last thing I remember is Dave Turbet turning the music up so loud that the floor starts to vibrate and still Bran doesn't wake up.

*

I have the shakes whilst cashing up. There's cigarette ash everywhere—in the coin counter, on the keyboard, I have to blow a small mound off my lap. I have not touched a drink for a week because I want to prove to myself that I can do without it.

When I'm done, I go out into the club where Bran, Gately, Tattoo Paul, the Fume, and Little Harry are laughing at Jordan Bone because he's fallen asleep again on the red sofa in the alcove by the fire exit. He looks almost angelic in the half-light, hands crossed over his belly. Paul takes a picture.

*

The next day, Tattoo Paul posts five pictures of Jordan Bone on Facebook, all of him asleep on various sofas, with the caption **DJ EURO PIGEON—COMING TO A SOFA NEAR YOU!**

*

Gately is out with Bran one Thursday and they come into Munks drunk from The Bellhop, and Gately goes behind the upstairs bar and logs into Facebook. The Fume and Bret are upstairs cleaning down when they realise that Gately, the stupid drunken bastard, has left himself logged in.

On Friday morning, when Gately is woken early by his son crying, severely hungover, he logs into Facebook and finds this written as his status.

Just found out that Alfie is not my son. Words cannot describe how I feel right now.

There are twenty-five comments.

Four people like this.

*

"I hope you two are proud of yourselves."

The Fume shrugs. Bret smiles uneasily. It's the lock-in after the night before.

"Well, serves him right for being out on the piss when he has a baby at home, doesn't it?" says Bret.

"Still," says Tanya, who came back last week and begged me to re-employ her, "it was a bit harsh. Anna is really upset about it."

"Don't worry," says Callie, "he's going to apologise…" she taps him on the knee—"aren't you, Bret?"

"Of course," says Bret. "I understand why Anna is upset—but I didn't mean to offend her."

"Whose idea actually was it?" says Georgie.

"Well, I typed the words. The Fume came up with the first bit. I added the second. And surely the people she should really be upset with are the four people who liked it?"

"You know that they had phone calls and messages throughout the night from various people."

"Fucking idiots," I say.

They all look at me.

"Well, why would you believe something like that when it is written on fucking Facebook? Why would you believe anything on that fucking site? Do these people have lives?"

*

Daniel is in one night with a load of equally camp-looking and over-enthusiastic Performing Art students, Blizzie and Georgie among them. They are all wearing fancy dress—a concept that I have never completely understood. Daniel is talking absolute crap to Mike and me on the door, some bullshit about what he's been doing this summer which involves singlehandedly running a pub in Basingstoke—I stop listening after the first ten seconds and only tune back in when he asks me if there are any shifts going.

"Damn, if you'd asked me yesterday, I could have said yes, but I've just hired somebody."

"Ah, shit, well, ok… if you ever need me, man, give me a call, yeah?"

"Absolutely."

He goes into the club. Kerry, who's on the till, says, "Who have you just hired?"

"Nobody. I just can't bear to listen to that guy talk as much shit as he does on a nightly basis."

Georgie comes out drunk with Blizzie and another girl. I stop them and ask the girl if she wants a job.

*

"You know that you two are public enemies numbers one and two."

"Yeah, so I've heard," says the Fume.

"But I've apologised…" says Bret. "Have you, Willy?"

"It wasn't me," he says, with a grin.

Bret is on his iPhone. "Listen to this—Gately's girl-friend has said in her status that she has just found out who did 'it' and she is shocked and upset. What the fuck? I barely know the girl. She then got over thirty comments. I'll read you the highlights."

"Oh god," I say, and shake my bottle of beer to see if it's empty.

"*Whoever did this deserves to burn in hell.*"

The Fume gives a high-pitched, Nelson-esque laugh.

"Hope you are both alright. The guy who did this is sick in the head!"

"Fuck me, what is wrong with people?"

"Wait for it… *when I find out who did this, I'm going to find them and chop them up into tiny pieces and make them suffer…* well, there we are, Willy, you and I need to go into hiding, mate."

"Well… you do. I'm in the clear."

I'm still shaking my head when I come back from the cellar with more beers.

*

I'm standing by the door till with Mike, Pete Bone and Stacie when we see a guy with long brown hair and a smart white shirt walking out of the club with a backpack on, an unlit cigarette between his lips, and an open bottle of red wine cradled in his arms. Mike grabs him as he comes through and flicks the bottle. It's glass.

"Sorry mate you can't have this in here."

"But it's mine."

"I'm confiscating it."

"No, you're not."

Mike tries to grab it off him but the guy won't let go— they wrestle the bottle back and forth and then the bloke slips and falls to the floor, but still refuses to let go. Mike stands over him for a moment, then says "Oh, fuck it," and lets him hold it, but bends his wrists round until the bottle is pointing over the guy's face. Then it's spilling over him, about three-quarters of a bottle of wine, and Mike's saying, "If you want the wine that fucking much you can have the fucking wine," and the guy is spluttering, his white shirt splattered red, until the bottle is empty.

He gets up and wipes his face. Mike hands him the bottle back, and he walks out, looking like he's been stabbed.

*

After Acoustic Array, I go next door for a quick pint before home and Gately is pissed in the bar with a load of his mates. I saw him busking this afternoon, howling some song in his high voice down by the abbey.

It takes a lot of control on my part, when I'm sitting quietly in the corner with a pint, not to go over to him and tell him to get the fuck home to his girlfriend and look after his baby.

*

There has been no resolution to the theft in the upstairs bar. Terry has passed all the evidence we have onto the police—blurry CCTV footage of a thief who could be anyone and a list of old names. It all amounts to nothing.

*

In my office with the Fume, going through the cash sheet from last night.

"Gately was pissed in The Bellhop again," I say.

The Fume shakes his head—he's had a haircut, chopped off his long dark locks, and he looks like a different man. He looks like a manager. "The guy is a fucking idiot," he says.

*

Meet the squaddy asleep in the left-hand cubicle of the Gents' toilets. The door is wide open, his trousers are around his ankles, he's completely fucking wasted, and his genitals are submerged—floating in the shitty water.

"He hasn't got any pubes," says Mike.

"He's going to get nob rot," I say.

It's getting on for the end of the night and we're trying to wake him up by pouring water over his head but he's out and not waking up for anything or anyone, and I'm vaguely aware that the music has stopped and everyone is leaving and still we're in here trying to wake this guy up. Sam and Mike squeeze into the cubicle and get him off the toilet—they lever him up, and with great difficulty, Mike gets behind him and tries to pull his jeans up while Sam holds him upright.

"He's gone fucking commando," says Mike.

"Fuck's going on here, lads?"

Pete 2 comes in and stands beside me, then gets his phone out and takes a picture of Mike trying to pull the squaddy's jeans up, looking like he's trying to do him from behind. Eventually, he gets them up over the guy's arse.

"Right, who's zipping him up then?" asks Mike. "Sam?"

"Fuck off."

"Well, I'm not doing it."

He's coming around now, leaning on the wall by the sinks, muttering—all we catch is the odd word.

"What's he saying?"

"Sounds like come home or cologne."

I hold the guy's face and try and look into his eyes. They flicker, half dead. "Mate, come on, you need to sober up, you can't get a taxi like this."

When he can stand properly, we walk him out of the club and I stay outside with him, wondering if he really will get nob rot, rolling us a cigarette each whilst we wait for his taxi. When it arrives, he's able to talk at least, and I watch him walk half straight down the steps, open the door and crawl in.

*

I'm at home for once when I get a text from Bret who's managing tonight.

Just went next door. Guess who was late for work and in there?

Gately?

Yep. He said he had forgiven me for the Frape.

How pissed was he?

Pissed.

Can he work?

He better. It's rammed.

*

Terry comes to me one afternoon and tells me that we had a complaint last night from one of the bands.

"What about?"

"A member of staff."

"Which one?"

"Their description was the one with blonde dreadlocks."

"Andrew Gately."

"Yes."

"What did he do?"

"Apparently, a member of the band went to the door to the downstairs bar to ask for some water, and Andrew slammed the door in his face and told him to fuck off."

"Right. What an idiot."

"Yes. Quite. Had he been drinking?"

"I had a night off. Bret was managing. I'll talk to him."

"Well, can you make it clear to young Andrew that he is on very thin ice?"

*

"Wait for it, wait for it…"

"Which window are you looking at?"

"The middle one, Sam, you twat… well, actually, I don't know which one you're looking at, you big gay!"

"There she is!"

"Jesus!"

"WAHEY!"

"Look at those hooters."

"She fucking loves it."

"Dirty tart."

"Just waitin' for somebody to go over there and give her a good seeing to."

When the place is dead and there are no punters to victimise, the bouncers need to find other forms of entertainment.

*

Meet the old Rastafarian beggar who roams the streets. He is a nasty piece of work—I have to tell him twice a week to stop bothering the smokers and the people in the queue outside the club. A week ago, he was set upon by a dozen or so men outside another club a little way along the road. The only person to come to his aid was Abasi, walking home after a night on the doors. The big bouncer hasn't a scratch on him, apart from one tiny blemish on the top of his bald head about the size of a ten pence piece.

When the other bouncers ask him why he helped the beggar, he just spreads his enormous arms. His huge bulk suddenly appears humble, kindly. Behind him on the counter are containers and containers of takeaway food that he gets delivered, free of charge, every night.

"He was on his own—what else could I do, man?"

"I'd have let the little cunt get the fuck kicked out of 'im," says Slicer. "In fact, I'd be doing the fucking kickin'."

*

Five o'clock the next afternoon—a Saturday. I'm not long awake, standing outside The Bellhop smoking a cigarette and drinking a pint to level my head when the pavement explodes. There is a low, growling noise, the sound of brick and mortar shifting, and on the walkway that runs parallel with the road, I see the paving stones shift. There's steam, then silence.

*

Cub is managing The Bellhop. The lights are off so she's lit candles. Music is playing from someone's iPhone. There are maybe twenty, thirty people in the pub.

"What do I do? What do I do?" she keeps saying.

I tell her to calm down. There is nothing she can do.

The fire brigade are here in numbers, swarming the walkway between Munks and The Bellhop and I've heard whispers that a cable has blown beneath the pavement on Gin Lane. Shortly after it happened, I went next door and tried the lights. The bulbs remained dark. The power sockets dead. This once great venue now completely powerless.

I look at my watch. Almost 7 pm. Tonight, Dave Abbott has organised a special night and the legend that is Grandmaster Flash is playing and the place is sold out. I'm supposed to open the doors at ten. He's arriving at eleven.

Outside, sirens are still wailing. I'm at the bar, listening to a group of guys playing guess the paedophile.

"Paul Daniels."

"That's a good shout. How about Des O'Connor?"

"Ooh, another good one. How about another Radio 1 DJ—Tony Blackburn?"

"Noel Edmunds. I'd say that tucking your jumper into your jeans is one hell of a giveaway."

"Ha—definitely."

"What about Ian Williams?"

Laughter that fades into silence.

"Hang on, he's not in here, is he?"

They look around shiftily at the faces over the candles, before going back to their drinks and lowering their voices.

*

The power comes back at 9:30, just as DJ Euro Pigeon, Harry D, and DJ Tim turn up early to set up. With big grins on their faces, they ask, "Is he here yet?"

By ten to ten, there's a queue to get in.

*

Little Harry comes upstairs to tell me that Gately has gone AWOL.

"He's what?"

"Gone."

"Where?"

"Well, he said he was going for a fag but he just hasn't come back. That was almost an hour ago."

"Who's on the bar?"

"Ellie—new girl."

"Fuck sake—you better get back down there. I'll sort out Andrew."

I go next door and he's not there. Outside there is no sign of him. Grandmaster Flash is scheduled to go on in half an hour and people are getting restless—there's hardly room to breathe. I go downstairs and it's packed. people are hanging over the bar trying to get served, practically throwing money at Little Harry and Ellie, some serving themselves and leaving notes on the bar.

I go into the cellar and find Andrew, sitting down on a barrel, asleep. He wakes up when I approach him.

"What are you doing?"

"Having a sleep. Tired."

"Mate, get the fuck out there!"

*

When I'm doing the following week's rota, Gately's name doesn't appear on it.

*

I'm watching Pete Bone lose it one night and thump some guy who's kicking off when I think—it's a good job this man doesn't drink.

*

I'm sitting next door having a pint with Harrison and Desmond because they're starting their European tour tomorrow when I realise that I've lost my keys. Not my house keys. No—Munks' keys. The master set. Keys to all the recently changed locks that Terry made a point of telling me cost him a lot of money. It's almost kicking out time and when all the customers are gone, The Bellhop staff help us look for them. I'm under a table when Desmond realises that he's lost his keys too, and when nothing is found under the tables, I go and check outside where I find Desmond's keys in Munks' studio doorway.

Half an hour later, we've stopped looking and are having another drink.

"What are you going to do?" asks Cub.

"Have a long, hard pray overnight and hope that tomorrow morning they turn up."

"And if they don't?"

"Anybody know a cheap locksmith?"

*

I find my keys the next morning—posted through the letterbox in a big white envelope with **THE MANAGER** written on it. There's a note inside which says: *Don't lose these. Like you have lost everything else. x*

*

I don't tell Terry. Something tells me this isn't the thief—who I have decided is one of two names on the list I sent Terry—and that the robbery was just done by an opportunist who kept an old key, acting on a whim. No, this is too personal. The handwriting belongs to a woman and there were no women on the list.

*

"Erm… why do I have no shifts this week?" asks Gately.

I'm sitting on the door till whilst Kerry goes for a fag. There's nobody around apart from Pete Bone who's on his phone—probably watching a Bruce Lee video or Liverpool highlights or something.

"I'm afraid that's something you're going to have to take up with Terry," I say.

"Why?"

"As I said—my hands are tied. You need to speak to Terry, mate."

His eyes are red like he's been crying and his little face looks so woebegone that I don't have the heart to sack him there and then.

*

Rick tells me he has a major problem.

"Here, look at this!" He shoves his phone in my face. On the screen is a picture of a penis.

"Rick, will you stop flashing pictures of your cock around the place."

He laughs and I walk away, reminding myself that this guy is also studying Forensic Science at university.

*

There is a huge tour bus parked on the street outside Munks and The Bellhop. A band called Vintage Trouble are playing and the night is sold out. Even Dom turns up and stays until just before midnight—any later and I'm sure he would turn into a pumpkin. After their gig, the band hang around, drinking with the customers, and at around 4 am, when we're shutting up, they invite a load of people over to their tour bus. I tell Tanya, Tattoo Paul, and Bran that I'll be over when I'm done cashing up but really I have no intention of joining them. All night I've been fighting the urge to collapse, fighting it by drinking pints and pints of energy drink, and soon after I've put the cash in the safe and locked up, I go outside. I can hear music and laughter from the tour bus. I turn away and walk off in the direction of home.

*

Managers have a spotted record in this place. During Ian's long and eventful tenure, he had a string of managers— thieves, substance abusers, and one guy who liked to fall asleep on the floor in the office and was sacked when Ian walked in and found him. And then there was Ian's sister Dorothy who painted the bleak and dark walls pink when Ian was on holiday. When he got back, he barred her.

*

Meet the camp guy at the upstairs bar drinking double vodka lime and sodas with a group of girls on a Thursday night. The place is full of students. I'm covering Bran whilst he goes for a fag, serving drinks at the end of the bar and listening to the camp guy talking to three girls about classes and modules and grades and other stuff, and when I get to him, he orders more vodka lime and sodas, gives me his card and when I bring the PDQ machine over, he says, "Erm, I was just wondering if I could reserve a table for Saturday?"

"What?"

"Can I reserve that table over there in the corner for Saturday night?" He puts his pin number in.

"Erm, no." He hands the PDQ machine back to me.

"Why not?"

"Because this is Munks, mate. You can't reserve tables." The machine spits his receipt out.

"Oh… well, it's just that I model for Gucci, and my agent is coming down to the city and well, I'd like to book that table over there."

"I told you," I give him his card and receipt for a round that came to the grand total of £7.50. "You can't reserve tables here. In case you hadn't noticed," and I look around at a bar where students are putting shots of vodka in their eyes and snorting Sambuca off the bar, "it's not that sort of place... darling."

*

It's no accident that the people who have left this place, either by choice or by being fired, have moved on to have better lives. I can recall a whole host of faces who walked out the door, and months, years later became teachers, lawyers, rock stars, writers, accountants. Last week, a guy called Alf Bates came in. Years ago, he got sacked for getting so pissed he couldn't work. I remember Harrison and Shelly had to cover for him—hide him in the cellar whilst one of them cleaned the upstairs bar and the other kept guard so the manager didn't find him—draped over the barrels, absolutely fucked. He's now a senior executive at a high street bank. I go to him for advice when I get into financial trouble, and, in return, I let him in for free.

*

The toilets in this place used to be upstairs where the bar is now. When I used to come in as a customer, long before I worked here, somebody used to periodically go into the Gents' and block the toilets. They would leak down onto the dance floor and people would dance, in their element, mouths raised and open to the sky, embracing the free shower, oblivious to the fact that they were dancing in other people's shitty water.

*

Chuchy… calling

I throw my phone across the room. On the other side of the curtains is the same false daylight that I walked home in this morning.

*

"Am I still barred?"

"'Fraid so, Chuch."

"Fuck sake. I need the money. I've had to get a real job."

"A real job?"

"Yeah."

"Where?"

"Loch Fyne—the seafood restaurant."

"Classy."

"Yeah, it's alright."

"Oh yeah, will you stop fucking ringing me when I'm asleep and waking me up?"

He takes his phone out—still the same one with the cracked screen.

"It's fucked," he says. "And it's probably because you're on my favourites list. I keep ringing my gran in the middle of the night as well. Last night, I was at Orwell's house at about 5 in the morning picking up a gram, chatting shit, fucked, when I hear this little voice coming from my pocket… *'Chris… Chris… are you there?'…*"

"Your poor gran."

"Nah, she's OK, bless her."

"Did you ever find out who was texting you those messages?"

"No, I didn't. I got another one the other day saying… well, here, let me find it… erm… yeah, spinning me out, mate, I don't know who the fuck it is—*Tonight I sat opposite you whilst you played your tunes and I fudding loved it…* and then ten kisses."

"Ten?"

"Yeah. What does ten kisses mean?"

"It means you need a restraining order, mate."

*

What is a face?

Something we are shown in the mirror when we choose to look, in a picture when somebody tags you on Facebook, or on the back page of your passport, if you have one.

But how can we truly know that what we see is what we look like? How do we know we don't look different the rest of the time?

*

Georgie is bored one day so she makes a list and tacks it to the wall by the door till:

THINGS PETE BONE DOESN'T EAT

- Sweets
- Kebabs
- Mushy stuff aka houmous
- Curry
- Sauces (apart from ketchup)
- Cheese
- Thais
- Indians
- Chinese
- Europeans
- Garlic
- Plastic bottle tops
- Butter!
- Booze
- Aniseed
- Brown sugar
- Radish

*

We're short on doormen one night so Mike gets Bill's brother Ed in. Polar opposite to Bill (the social recluse and virgin), Ed has difficulty restraining himself sexually. He's a bodybuilder with a day job as a gym instructor.

I come back inside from having a smoke, go into the staff toilets upstairs and open the door to find Ed standing there, trousers around his ankles, pumping away furiously. He turns and looks at me with red, hooded eyes.

"For fuck's sake, Ed!"

I shut the door.

Five minutes later he comes out.

"Good wank, Ed?" says Mike, laughing.

"Not bad."

"Ed—not at work, mate," I say. "And at least lock the bloody door."

"Sorry—it's the testosterone."

Ed goes outside. Mike is still laughing. I crack a smile and Mike says, "Bill told me he got a disciplinary at work once for wanking on the job."

*

Wednesday night and Munks is shut. We cordon off a private room next door for Bran's birthday—he's twenty-eight. I buy him shots of Tuaca whenever I go to the bar and he does well until around 10 pm when his dubstep fanatic proper gangster homeboys, or as I think of them— cardboard cut-out cunts—turn up with their snapback caps and chunky trainers and chains. One of them rolls a joint which, as usual, destroys Bran's mind, and when The Bellhop closes, we make a human chariot to transport him to a club down the road where, for some reason, they let him in. We put him in a corner and he sits with his eyes pointing in different directions, muttering to himself in Spanish and punching thin air.

*

I'm watching a guy through the window as he kicks the front door, going absolutely crazy.

"GIVE ME MY FUCKING COAT BACK!"

"IT'S NOT FUCKING HERE!" I shout back.

"YES, IT IS!"

He carries on kicking. His eyes have a glare to them. I hear wood splinter.

It's 4:45. All the bouncers have gone home and this guy has been outside for forty-five minutes, constantly ringing the club phone, banging on all the windows and doors, and now he's trying to force his way back in.

"Are we sure his coat isn't in there?" I say to Blizzie, Georgie, and Ellie who are standing by the door till behind me, all holding hands.

"Yeah," says Blizzie. "I only took three coats all night and they were all girls' ones."

"Fuck's sake."

Sweat is pouring down the guy's face. He grits his teeth, roars, and does a flying kick at the door which leaves it shaking.

I take my phone out and dial 999. The guy is significantly bigger than I am and I doubt I could fight him on my own.

He stops kicking the door when he sees the phone at my ear.

"Hello—yeah, I'm calling from Munks' nightclub. Yes, yes, I'm sorry, it's me again. I have a man trying to kick his way through the front door… OK… you're on your way… thank you."

A few seconds later, he gives me the finger and leaves.

*

The next day, I get this email:

Dear Munks

This is a quick email just to say that I am sorry for the damage I caused to your front door last night in an attempt to retrieve my coat from your cloakroom. As it happened, a friend of mine had taken my coat home earlier in the night and forgot to tell me. I will of course pay for any damage that I caused.

Humbly yours,
Kevin Hodge

*

I get the door fixed and send him the bill. I neglect to tell Terry as I know he will want to press charges. I feel that every now and then, somebody deserves to be let off.

*

I get a phone call at 11 pm on a Saturday from somebody who tells me a guy called Little Chris is on his way and is coming to the club.

"Who?" I ask.

"Little Chris. He'll be there around one o'clock."

"Right."

I put the phone down and ask Tanya and the bouncers if they know who Little Chris is.

"Yeah," says Pete Bone, "he's that little shit who was on X Factor or something."

"Yeah," says Tanya, "he's only like 17."

"17?" says Mike. "Well, he can't come in then, can he?"

At 1:30 a Mercedes with blacked-out windows pull up on the kerb opposite. We stand outside and watch as a kid wearing a baseball cap and a baggy green hoody gets out, followed by a gaggle of girls and four or five big guys wearing dark suits and glasses. They climb the steps up to the walkway and approach the door.

"Can I help?" asks Mike.

A small man holding a Filofax, who I didn't notice before, breaks off from the entourage and comes forward. Presumably, the manager or agent or something.

"Hi," he says, "erm, I called up earlier to say that we'd be coming in."

"Did you?" says Mike.

"Er yes, this is Little Chris."

"Yo," and Little Chris holds out his fist for Mike.

Mike looks at him, ignores the peace fist, and says, "He's not coming in."

"Erm, what?" says Little Chris's manager.

"He's not coming in."

"Why not? We called—"

"I don't care if you called all the way from China, he's not coming in because he's underage."

"Oh… right."

"But if the young ladies would like to get their IDs out, I would have no problem letting them in if they're old enough, and you gentlemen, of course…"

The big guys in glasses don't move. I wonder if they have one brain between them.

A moment later they're going back down the steps and I hear Little Chris say, "I've heard this place sucks anyway," and they get back in the Mercedes and drive off.

*

After decades of not believing in miracles, one happens.

Bran moves out of his mum's house.

But he still goes back there most nights, even at five in the morning after work, rather than sleep in the flat he now shares with the Fume, which is only two minutes from Munks.

It's early evening and I'm having a drink on the tables outside The Bellhop with the Fume. He tells me that every few weeks, Bran comes into work and says he has some money for him and gives him about £200 (sometimes a little more and sometimes a little less)—his contribution to rent and bills.

"That's most of his wages," I say, shaking my head, still unable to comprehend the man I've known for a decade.

"Exactly," says the Fume. "It's perfect really—all the bills and rent go out of my account, and I just live on what he pays me."

"So why the hell doesn't he actually sleep in the flat he's paying rent for?"

The Fume shrugs, "His excuse is that I don't have the internet."

"So, he can't watch porn."

We smoke, breaking into laughter at intervals. I try to call Bran a couple of times but it's pointless—it goes to answerphone because he's still asleep.

*

Dom has organised an underage battle of the bands night. The place is full of kids, and a few overagers who get a wristband on the way in.

I'm bored so I go on the bar upstairs with Bran and let the Fume manage the children and the parents. One kid in particular, Asian and wearing a snapback cap and chunky gold necklace, keeps coming up to the bar and asking for a drink.

"You don't have a wristband, mate," we keep telling him, and he gets all shirty every time we turn him away.

Half an hour later, he comes up to the bar and puts down an empty plastic bottle of Beck's, smiles at us, walks away and does that retarded hand thing that gangsters do.

"Little prick," I say. I leave the bar and go and tell the staff downstairs that if they see anybody give the little shit a drink, they're to come and find me. I also give Mike a heads-up.

Fifteen minutes later, the kid comes back with another empty bottle.

"Listen, mate," I say. "We know what you're doing. If I see you with a drink in your hand again, you will be thrown out."

"Fuck off," he says and walks away.

*

Half an hour later, I see him leaning against the wall downstairs, swigging from a bottle of beer, laughing with his mates. I go and get Mike and Stacie and they drag the little bastard out. He struggles—"Get the fuck off of me! I'll fucking do you!" and they chuck him out onto the street.

*

Twenty minutes later, just as we're closing, Mike comes running up to the bar and I follow him to the front door which he and Stacie, the only two bouncers on duty, have locked. A group of people are outside—what looks like the underage kid's whole family—and they are shouting and gesticulating at us through the window. Then they start throwing rubbish and all sorts of crap at the window. I see the remnants of a kebab slide down the glass leaving a trail of chili sauce and mayonnaise.

One woman, presumably the kid's mother, is shrieking, looking at me, constantly thrusting her hands up into the air, "I'M GONNA BURN THIS MOTHERFUCKING PLACE DOWN! WHAT? YOU NEVER SEEN AN ASIAN WOMAN GET ANGRY BEFORE?"

A group of girls are behind us who must have been in the toilets when we closed the doors. The look scared and as asking if it's safe to go home.

I tell the Fume to phone the police, Mike to hold the fort, and I lead the girls to the fire exit at the side of the building. I open the door, see the street is empty, and usher them through. In the open air, the threats of the Asian family aren't as muffled and the mother's shrieking is far worse, and I wait until the girls have vanished around the corner safely before shutting and bolting the door.

*

When the police arrive—two men and a woman—the family gather around them, shouting louder, jumping up and down. I hear the words "Motherfuckers" and "Player haters," and the mother is squaring up to the female officer, and then after a few minutes of more shouting and swearing and jabbing at us on the other side of the glass, she strides away, still raving. Her son is leaning on the railings, smoking with his friends, and she grabs his hand as she passes and drags him away. And once the matriarch has gone, it's not long before the rest of them, after a final threat and a few pistol gestures to the head, gradually move on too.

I look at Mike, who's sweating and shaking his head, and he says, "That's what you get these days for trying to uphold the law."

*

There is a band from Israel playing called The Bohemians and they have drawn a large crowd. I stand on the edge with Mike, who's looking at his phone.

One moment the drummer is banging on the drum kit, and the next the drum kit is on fire.

I watch it burn—stare deep into the flames for what seems like a long time and imagine the pain of being burnt alive.

Then I realise it's really happening and tap Mike on the shoulder.

"What?"

"Erm, the drum kit is on fire."

"Jesus."

He stands there and watches the flames for a few seconds—they've probably been going for almost a minute now—before going to get a fire extinguisher. The band is still playing as if nothing unusual is happening, but people in the crowd are looking at each other and pointing. Jeff the sound man is waving to get my attention. When Mike comes back, it's still burning, and he says, "Ten seconds more, if they don't put it out…"

Ten seconds later, just as he pushes through the edge of the dance floor, the fire is extinguished.

But I can still see the flames on the inside of my eyelids for a long time afterwards.

*

"Did you see Alf Bates when he came in last week?" asks Bran.

"Yeah," I say, and turn to the Fume, Blizzie and Little Harry to explain that Alf used to work here.

"Great guy," says Bran. "Funny as fuck."

"Do you remember how he got his job?" I ask. "I was clearing up the old upstairs bar and he's standing there, fucked, having a piss up against it, and I'm like 'What the fuck are you doing?' and he just says 'Having a piss.' Next day—the manager at the time, John, gave him a job."

"Did he know about him pissing against the bar?" says Little Harry.

"I never mentioned it. As Bran said, Alf was a great guy."

"He once put his cock in a shot glass," says Bran, laughing.

"What?" says the Fume.

"Seriously?" says Blizzie.

"Well, this guy was being a right fucking arsehole to Alf on the bar, a proper dick, and Alf says to me 'I bet that guy will have a shot in the next hour', and goes round the corner and rubs his knob in this glass. Then he brings it round and puts it on an empty shelf. An hour later, the guy orders a shot of Sambuca or something and Alf uses that one."

"Yeah," I say, "I remember that. The guy winced as it went down and asked what flavour Sambuca it was."

I leave them laughing and go back to the office to start cashing up, but before I do, I go on Internet Explorer and look at the Google search bar:

my garage tried to kill me
had a great night now suffering
psycho ex-girlfriend

*

I'm doing last week's wages in my office when I get an email from Harrison who's on tour somewhere in Europe. He's attached a YouTube link and written—*Check this out. Unbelievable. Hope all is good there, babes x*

I click on it. It's titled MY VIDEO NASTIES REVIEW 2012, 69 List—Part 1 of 3.

I press play and wait for it to buffer, wondering what the hell is about to happen.

The video starts and I see a living room—dark sofa, white walls, a kitchen in the background. Pete Bone sits down on the sofa, facing the camera. He's wearing a black Elliot Minor Solaris hoody and blue Adidas joggers. He exhales and says, in his thick West Country accent:

"Hi guys, I'm just going to do a few more reviews of Nasties. I did the 38 last time, so I'm just going to stick with a few others, what I've got on the other list, the 69 list, and er, gonna start with *Living Dead in the Manchester Morgue*, which is also *Let Sleeping Corpses Lie*, Jorge Grau's

1974 zombie film, got it in the American uncut tin, well worth havin', as the tins are, there's a few cards n that in there, a little morgue tag, and obviously the DVD. A good one, and well worth addin' to the collection."

He puts the DVD down and picks up another.

"Next, we've got *Eaten Alive*, also called *Death Trap* in this country, Toby Hooper, same person who did *Texas Chainsaw Massacre*, good movie, well worth havin', and erm, uncut now, and uncut over here now as far as I know. One of the ones that Mary Whitehouse took a dislike to, back in the day, not that she's ever seen it, I don't think she's seen any of them, but erm, well worth havin'. The story's good. And some good killin' in it. Well worth havin'."

He picks up another.

"Next is a film called *Stage Fright*, erm, some good gore n that in this…"

This goes on for another twelve minutes.

My Bloody Valentine
Pieces
Maniac
Evil Dead
Cut and Run
The Cannibal Holocaust
Beyond the Darkness
The New York Ripper
Torso
The Toolbox Murders

Until:

"Finally, now this isn't strictly a nasty, but I'm going to review it anyway cos it's well worth havin'. *Class of 1984*, an early 80s film, uncut, tin version this one. I do believe I have three versions of this, the English one and the French one cos the French one was the only version available when I wanted it. I've been told the English version is a little bit trimmed on the rape scene, I'm not sure, I couldn't tell much difference when I watched it… but I picked this one up pretty cheap, still sealed as well, still sealed in the cellophane and I think I'll leave it that way as I don't particularly need to watch this version… right, that's it for now. If you want to leave a comment about any of these films, please leave a comment, and erm, thank you for listening and I'll see you again."

And I stare at the screen, agog, occasionally breaking into fits of laughter, because finally, I know what this man does when he's not here.

*

I see Gately periodically in the pub next door, drunk, and on the streets, strumming his guitar and singing with his eyes shut, his dreads swinging from side to side as he bounces to his own music. He also keeps coming into the club expecting to still get in for free to see the people who are the real reason why he lost his job. He comes up to me and reels off a load of shit about Terry, says how he's going to take him to court for wrongful dismissal, and I ask him if he has another job yet and he says no, but the band is about to take off, they're touring soon and he's been busking lots, and all the while I just want to tell him to get the fuck home and look after his son.

*

"You know, Gately says he's going to take Terry to court for wrongful dismissal," I say to the Fume. We're sitting outside The Bellhop, wearing coats, shivering. The weather is getting cold again.

"That kid needs a reality check—does he know what a zero-hour contract is?"

"I know—he's also oblivious to the fact that I stopped giving him shifts because no one wanted to work with him."

We both roll another cigarette.

"How do they survive financially?" I say, passing him my lighter.

"I think his dad's a barrister," he says.

"Yeah, that would help."

*

Meet the ambulance people. They have the downstairs bar to themselves on a Friday night at 11 pm. There are three of them—Mary, Carrie and Frank the Scouser who's gay and came onto me a few years ago by barking at me like a dog. Mary then asked me if I was single and said that her friend fancied me. I thought she meant Carrie but it turned out to be Frank, who, when he isn't impersonating a dog, is a nice chap. He buys me a drink every time they come in and winks at me and asks if I'm still straight.

Frank and Carrie are currently dancing to 'Rapper's Delight' on the empty dance floor. I'm behind the bar talking to Mary who asks, "Were you OK the other night?"

"What?"

"You don't remember, do you?"

"That depends on what it is."

"You were walking home… Tuesday night, and we were driving past and Carrie saw you, said we better stop and see if you were OK because you were stumbling along, you couldn't walk straight, and then you tripped and fell into the gutter."

"Are you sure it was me?"

"Absolutely. We stopped and got out to see if you were OK. We had about a five-minute conversation. You were smiling for most of it. I gave you a cigarette because you couldn't find your tobacco."

"Really?"

"Yeah, and then you said 'I'm going home now.' I told you to try and stay on the pavement, and you tootled off."

I scratch my head, "Seems like I owe you three a shot then," and I grab the bottle of Tuaca and pour out four.

*

Going through the incident report book because I'm bored of the internet and it's early on a Thursday and there's nobody in. There are pages and pages of handwritten notes—Dirt Literature detailing decades of shady happenings in the Kingdom of Doom at the drunken hour. I only put it down to open my bottom drawer, find the passport and look at Henrietta Mary's picture again, at the words on the last page, and even though it's over an hour since Kyle played 'Psycho Killer' by the Talking Heads, I've been hearing it in my head ever since, sitting here, wondering—is this what love really is? Or is it something completely different?

*

I'm standing in the doorway of the Ladies' toilets looking in. 'Sinnerman' by Nina Simone is playing so loudly that I reach up to check if I'm wearing headphones. I'm not. The music is coming from the club. Then I look down and realise I'm naked. There's heat on my back. I turn and look back through the door, out into an inferno that stares right back at me. I see the lipstick on the wall, and the names. The ceiling burns, someone has written the words **A BIT TRIMMED ON THE RAPE SCENE** *in red on the mirror, the room is smokeless, my feet are stuck to the floor, bloody footprints lead up to the four cubicle doors—all shut. I approach the first and open the door. It is empty. There's blood in the toilet, little splashes on the white plastic seat, a smiley face drawn on the green wall, and below that, lines of cocaine on the cistern lid. I shut the door and go to the next. More blood, more cocaine on the cistern lid, but there are also two severed hands on the floor—pale, supple, female, with bracelets still* *on the wrists. In the third is a pair of maimed legs wearing torn tights, they've been stuck in the toilet like somebody has tried to flush them away. And in the fourth is a girl wearing a David Bowie t-shirt and nothing else. Her legs and her hands have been cut off. She is collapsed on the toilet seat and she stares at me, butchered arms reaching out as she says, "Why did you keep my passport?"*

I turn around and see her words written on the mirror and they're dripping with blood.

*

When I wake up, I'm standing opposite my building, staring at the flames behind the windows and the smoke unfurling in the air. I'm naked. Sirens in the distance.

*

Due to unfortunate circumstances, I am now living upstairs in The Bellhop. The fire wasn't in my flat itself (it was in the one below—some strung-out junkie fell asleep smoking a cigarette) but enough smoke damage was caused for me to have to move out. Not that I own an awful lot of things. A lot of vinyl. A dozen books. A few bottles. Clothes. Lots of shoes, most of them with the soles destroyed. In two trips, I move everything into the room next door to Luke and then we go downstairs for a pint.

*

Saturday night, almost 1 am and we have less than a hundred people in. That's according to the counter—I walk through the club and count less than fifty.

"Well, this is fucking shit," says Mike.

"Where is everybody?" asks Kerry.

"Fuck knows. Not in here."

I go next door and find the bar is packed. I look up at the board.

SHOT OF THE WEEK
THE JABBERWOCKY
55% and deadly
"And hast thou slain the Jabberwock?"

Luke brings over two Jabberwockies and I tilt mine back and slay the thing. I almost cough up blood on my way back to Munks.

*

Some staff let me down and I find myself frantically texting people at 11 pm but no one replies, and I'm leaning on the upstairs bar, swearing and wondering why I ever employed such a useless bunch of reprobates, but then Bret comes upstairs from setting up the downstairs bar and says that Callie will probably work for a one-off. He goes off up the hill to their flat to get her and puts her on the door till. She sits there all night, smiling, beautiful, far too good for this place, every guy that comes in flirting with her, Bret popping up from downstairs every twenty minutes to check on her, and I feel guilty because Slicer is on the door and his presence always causes the bouncers to be much more crude and offensive than usual.

*

Cashing up by candlelight—power cuts have been hitting the street all night. I have to fill in the spreadsheet by hand which is no mean feat and takes a lot of brainpower, and when I'm done, I sit back and think what is the fucking point. Terry never looks at the bloody things—the figures, the numbers, the facts—he's only interested in the money.

I light a cigarette, open my bottom drawer and take out the dead passport. I pull out my phone and dial the number written in it.

"The number you have called has not been recognised."

I hang up.

*

Candy (Chuchy) Fact ended when I barred Chuchy so Wednesday has remained a non-event since then, which I don't mind because it means an extra night off, not that I do much apart from sit in The Bellhop and drink. But occasionally, an outside promoter will come in and run a night, such as this one—a group of fashion students doing a charity club gig. One of them is Baby Gary who wears a beanie hat to cover up caveman hair—he used to work here and used to go out with Cub. He DJs the night with another beanie-hat-wearing guy who takes his music seriously—they play a mixture of funky tunes and house music for a handful of people grouped around the downstairs bar. The Beanie Hat DJs tend to get carried away with the smoke machine and send it pouring out onto the empty dance floor so I have to go and tell Baby to take it easy. Last time they were here, they set off the smoke alarms and we had to evacuate.

Half an hour later, I'm upstairs talking to Mike and Pete Bone on the doors when the smoke alarms go off.

"Oh, for fuck's sake," says Mike, "not again!" We go downstairs. The place is a pit of smoke. Mike heads to the bar to tell the customers and the bar staff to evacuate. I go to the DJ booth. Baby Gary—headphones on, head bobbing, eyes down—is working his magic on the decks. His mate is leaning against the wall, drinking a pint, also bobbing his head. Finally, after lots of shouting and gesticulating, I get his attention.

"WHAT?" he says, cupping an ear.

"THE FIRE ALARMS ARE GOING OFF!"

"WHAT?"

What the fuck is wrong with people?

"I SAID—TELL HIM TO TURN IT OFF! THE FIRE ALARMS ARE GOING OFF!"

The kid looks offended. "BUT HE'S IN THE MID-DLE OF A MIX!"

"THE FUCKING BUILDING IS ON FIRE!" I bellow and grab a handful of wires from the PA system and yank them out.

The music stops. Baby Gary looks up.

"What's going on?"

*

Another Saturday night in the Kingdom of Doom—a story that is getting all too familiar. I walk through the almost empty club, remembering a time when the place used to be packed every night of the week. Now it's only Dave's Cheese Night that gets more than a few hundred through the door, and even that seems quiet compared to what it once was. As for Kyle's Empire night, it is dying—slowly, painfully, all the student regulars have graduated and moved on to other cities. Last week, Mitch had to try and make the place look busy with only twenty people.

I go to the cloakroom and sit with Tattoo Paul for a while and eat his chocolates. He has no coats.

"The question," he says, "is how much longer T-WAT is going to last before he goes under and the place shuts down."

"I don't think Ian will ever let that happen," I say. "Munks has been here too long."

*

Halloween, and I'm next door with the ghouls and the ghosts. It's dark outside and people are pissed even though it's only 5 pm. I'm at the bar alone, there are skulls on the beer pumps and bats hanging from the roof. I'm staring at the weird picture of David Bowie on the wall by the Jack Daniel's bottle, and drinking a shandy because I'm still a bit shaky after last night and this night has the prospect of being a long and arduous one…

Cub has a girl in to paint faces and some guy goes over to her and asks if she can do him a Jimmy Saville, and I can only half smother a laugh. I'm listening to a noisy group around the corner where the joker came from—they're making odd slapping sounds interspersed with laughter and raucous cheers. I look up from my shandy to see Chuchy come through the door. He's wearing a black suit, white shirt, and red tie—it's the smartest I've ever seen him. He has a satchel over his shoulder which has his Mac and other equipment in it.

"Where you off to, Chuch?"

"Doing a Halloween party," he says.

"You look good."

"Here, check out what I'll look like later," and he pulls his iPhone out and shows me a picture of himself with blood dripping from his mouth.

"Nice."

"Here—happy Halloween," and he gives me a MOAM and leaves before I can ask him why he's suddenly stopped calling me in the middle of the night.

Cub appears from the little manager's office at the top of the stairs that lead down into the cellar bar. She comes up to me, puts a hand on my arm, and says, "Erm… Claire is coming in later. She's back in town for the weekend. I thought you should know."

I nod. She goes behind the bar.

I go to the Gents' and the urinals are busy so I go into the empty cubicle, shut and lock the door. Sit down. Put my head in my hands. When I'm done, I stand staring at the inside of the cubicle door because there it is, written in the same hand as it is in the toilets next door—**04:20?**

I order a large Havana Club and Coke and sit and wonder where I'll be next Halloween. Still here? Same job, same city, same life, or even—non-life?

But maybe the question I should be asking is not *where* I'm going to be but *who* I'm going to be.

*

It's 7:30 in the evening when I wake up—hungry, thirsty, still in my clothes and with no idea where, or even who I am. Stuck on my mirror are magazine cuttings of slasher villains—Freddy Krueger, The Miner, Jigsaw, Michael Myers, Leatherface, Norman Bates—black sharpie lines connecting them like a tube map, and big question mark in the middle. Then I see that I have the word **DISBOSOM** written on my hand and I have no idea why it's there or what it means.

*

The night the clocks go back—a strange night when you're in this business. The police come round at midnight, going into all the places along Gin Lane and checking bars and clubs will be shutting according to the old time—not taking advantage of an extra hour's trading. They've only just started doing this in the last couple of years. Before that, they didn't give a fuck.

People come up to me all night, asking if they get an extra hour's drinking. I smile, shake my head, and break the bad news.

*

The first good, really busy night for a long, long time and it is blemished by the arrival of local gangsters.

First, they refuse to pay. I'm standing at the entrance by the door till, wielding the stamp. The biggest one is called Johno. He has a shaven head and a flesh tube in his right ear, and when Kerry asks them for £6 each he smiles and says, "I've never paid to get in here, darling'."

Kerry looks at Mike, who shrugs and looks at me as if to say—*your call*.

I unfold my arms, look at Johno and say, "Charge these guys £3 each, Kerry."

Johno smiles and for a second I think he's going to kick off—he's reaching into his jacket pocket, and I see Mike brace himself, but it's a wad of £20 notes he pulls out, not a gun. He flicks through them, there's easily a thousand pounds there, gives Kerry one of them and he and his guys come in. I make a point of stamping their wrists as they pass me.

"When's Bas in, Mike?"
"Midnight."
"Get him here early if you can."

*

The mood changes as soon as they enter. What was a chilled-out, last Friday of the month vibe, becomes still, silent, uneasy. People know who they are. Euro Pigeon is DJing upstairs and he puts on some Jurassic 5. They stand at the upstairs bar and I watch from a distance as they drink large Jack Daniel's and Cokes. Johno greets Bran like an old friend and nods at the Fume, saying, "Who's the newbie?"

Bran's face doesn't relax until Johno lets go of his hand.

*

Abasi leaves his shift at the bar down the road early and comes in at 11.

"What's the problem?" he says.

"Local gangsters."

"Ah, not those guys. Had major trouble in Red Rooms with them last month."

"What happened?"

"One of them stole a bottle of vodka. Fights. Drugs. Trouble."

"You ban them?"

He laughs, "No chance. The boss knows better than to think he has the power to do that."

*

Mike and I have been monitoring them all night. They take over the upstairs bar and turn it into their private VIP area. Have Bran and the Fume make cocktails even though we don't serve cocktails. Have Jordy Bone play whatever they want to listen to. Around 1.30, they break off and some of them go downstairs, others outside to smoke.

Then, just before 2 am, the inevitable happens.

I'm walking downstairs to get some change for the door till, dodging around the pissheads, when I see Tanya, who has been in the cloakroom all night, stumbling, holding her head at the bottom of the stairs. I dash down and put a hand on her shoulder, "What happened? You OK?"

She's crying. "The big bald fucker punched me in the head."

"He did what?! What happened?"

"The girl with him was being a bitch to my friend, and when I tried to step in and defend her, he hit me."

"Right. Go upstairs to the door till. I'll shut the cloakroom."

I shut the cloakroom and call Mike on the radio, tell him what happened.

All five bouncers approach Johno—he's standing laughing at the bar, a girl at his arm who has a hideous orange tan and wears black leather boots.

"Johno," says Mike, "I'm going to have to ask you to leave, mate."

"What?"

"You heard me."

"Can I finish my drink first?"

Mike twitches, "If you're quick."

He's holding a full pint of Grolsch and suddenly he tips his head back and downs it in about three seconds. He wipes the froth from his lip and belches.

"OK—I'm going."

People try not to stare as we escort him up the stairs and out of the door. His girl goes with him. When he's outside, I say, "You know I'm going to have to ban you, Johno."

He smiles and says, "Everyone knows this place is going bust anyway," before walking away in the direction of The Bellhop, the girl with the orange face on his arm.

*

At the end of the night, several large vodkas and a few beers down already, I go to the Gents' and see, above the urinals, some new graffiti on the wall:

THE MANAGER OF THIS SHIT HOLE IS A DEAD MAN

*

The night after the gangsters, and Mike and I are drinking Vodka and Cokes in my office after we've closed.

"Well, I don't know about you, mate, but they can make all the fucking threats in the world, but that prick is not setting foot in the club as long as I'm the manager."

He smiles and nods. "I'm glad we're on the same page."

I sip my vodka, letting only a trickle go down my throat. Cough. Taste blood. My hand shakes. We both watch the dark liquid tremor.

"Are you OK, mate?"

"Fine mate, absolutely fine. Just tired. Very tired."

He nods, but he's still frowning.

*

It's approaching 2 am and we hardly have any customers. I've already shut the upstairs bar and now I'm downstairs sitting in the alcove with Bret, watching the morons dance to 'We Found Love' by Rihanna.

He tells me that next week will be his last week.

I nod, "We'll miss you. Where are you going?"

"I don't know yet. I think I need a normal job for a while. I've done this job as long as I can."

I nod again, envious. "A normal job?"

"Yeah, whatever that means."

"Just until you write your bestseller?"

He smiles, "It's in the making."

We drink our beers and look over at the bar. Little Harry, Georgie, and Tanya are messing around taking pictures of each other in Jack Daniel's t-shirts that we had delivered last week along with lots of other promotional crap.

"Well, it's been a pleasure to sweat by your side," I say.

"Likewise."

We watch a guy wearing a white shirt leap around on the dance floor like he's jumping an invisible skipping rope. He trips and pulls a girl over. She slaps him and walks off in the direction of the Ladies'.

"You know what," I say, "you should write a novel about this place. Even I would read it."

"Stacie told me the same thing on my first shift here."

"Well?"

"I may have a few ideas."

The song ends and the morons are caught mid-dance. Skipping Guy is now spilling his drink down his front, shuffling his feet in a sideways moonwalk to Flo Rida's 'Let it Roll'.

"The only thing I know for sure right now," he says, a strange, faraway look on his face, "is that it's going to be written from the perspective of the manager."

I finish my beer.

"You should call it *The Rum Diary*," I say.

"Already been done. You don't read enough, mate."

"I don't have the time."

*

There is a woman who comes into the club periodically, goes into the Ladies' toilets and does her business into a pint cup. Then she draws a smiley face and a kiss in lipstick on the outside of the cup and leaves it by the sinks. It always happens on a Thursday night. I have trawled through the CCTV footage many times for signs of this woman, trying to catch her identity, but for now, she remains a ghost.

*

This morning, I received this letter through the door:

> To Munks Nightclub, the manager, owner and staff
>
> I live in the row of houses opposite your Nightclub. Last Saturday, my elderly husband and I were kept awake until almost 5 in the morning by the people outside your club, who were making a horrendous amount of noise. It really is not on! We will be making a formal complaint to the council.
>
> Yours,
> RESIDENTS OF GIN LANE

We get three or four of these a year. As do The Bellhop, who have started tacking theirs to the wall behind the bar. Some are more aggressive than others. Nothing ever comes of these complaints. I'm afraid the only answer to them is—don't live next door to a nightclub.

*

Alone in the club. We took a fair amount of money tonight and it's taking longer than usual to make sense of it. The spreadsheet is playing tricks on me, the hours are rolling around far too quickly, the ashtray is full, I'm having hunger pangs, sweating, my breath is too quick, I get up six times in twenty minutes to check all the doors are locked, and when I get up a seventh time, I have one hand on the door handle before everything slips into black.

*

I'm holed up in my room, wearing two hoodies and jogging bottoms, watching endless TV. People keep coming upstairs to visit me—Cub and Bret are here at the moment.

"Callie says she hopes you feel better soon," says Bret.

"Ahh, tell her thanks, mate."

I'm going through the texts on my phone. Lots from the staff, even one from Terry (*Take as much time off as you need*), and one from my mother saying she'll call me tomorrow morning.

And this one—

Heard what happened. Hope you are OK. Maybe now you will realise. C x

I left the hospital two days ago and I've only just stopped shaking.

*

I listen to my mother's long answerphone message over and over and over again. It never changes. Every word stays the same. My only blessing is that she no longer lives in this country.

I was awake when she called, lying in bed, looking at the screen, seeing the words *Mother Calling* and waiting for it to stop.

How do you tell somebody that you have been abusing the kidney that they gave you to save your life the first time?

*

Back at work—people tell me I'm looking better. I smile and tell them I'm OK. The same can't be said for Terry's business. It's Saturday night and we have less than fifty people through the door.

*

I don't touch a drink for two weeks. Then I start again, slowly, just socially, drinking only shandies. No rum. No spirits. Definitely no shots of the week. I've decided my spiritual experience is over and, to be frank, it almost killed me. In a place like this, God is well and truly dead.

*

I have another text message from my mother:
You are welcome here anytime, don't forget that. X

*

11:30 am. I've just finished the paperwork and I'm banging on the side door of Yhe Bellhop, waiting for Cub to let me back in. Then I sit at the bar and ask her for a double Vodka and Lemonade, and a double JD and Coke.

I drink the vodka slowly. The date is November 23rd. My father's birthday. I ask Cub if she can put on Bob Dylan's 'Forever Young'. I leave the JD untouched, just sitting there, all day, whilst I drink a further half a dozen vodkas, just to remind myself that my father walked this earth but now he is gone.

*

I'm on the door till on a Saturday night because we're short-staffed, the number on the clicker is 72 and I look up to see Ian in the doorway, wearing his usual shorts and sandals.

"Ian," says Mike.

"Evening," he says. He's holding something in his hands. Paper. He walks up to the door till and puts it on the counter. I look down at the document. The words *Breaking the terms of lease* are repeated throughout.

"So, I suppose the inevitable is happening," I murmur.

"Tonight," says Ian, "you will take all the tills as usual, at the usual time, but you will pay all your staff's wages for this week in cash. If you read through this contract, everything will make sense."

I look up. "OK. And what happens then?"

"I have a locksmith coming in at 4:30 am to change the locks."

"And after that?"

"I'll be in touch."

*

The next day, I call an impromptu staff meeting in The Bellhop. I have a rucksack with me that contains almost two and a half grand in cash, divided up into wage packets, which I hand out to them. Then I explain what's happening.

Afterwards, I look at my phone and find I have twenty-five missed calls from Terry.

*

Signs appear in the windows of the café on Monday morning:

NOTICE FROM THE FREEHOLDER
OF THIS PROPERTY

- I act in my capacity as trustee of IM Williams SIPP (continued) 45667 the entity which is the freeholder and landlord of this property

- On Sunday 2nd December 2012, I re-entered the property and forfeited the lease that was granted to MUNKS Ltd (Company (continued) 31220332)

- I did this under clauses 36.1 a, b and c (iii) of the said lease which gives the right to enter the property and 36.2 which allows forfeiture of the lease

- Terry Watson or his agents or any agent of the former tenant company will be considered to be entering the property illegally and without the right to enter if they do so

Any queries relating to the following notice should be addressed to Ian Williams—07659577939 or emailed to ian@iwilliamsvenues.com

*

Terry spends the whole of Monday morning calling me. I ignore him. The club remains closed. All over Facebook, people are asking if it's true that Munks is closing down.

I sit upstairs in the kitchen above the pub with a crate of beer, watching meaningless television, listening to classical music, and staring at the photo in Henrietta Mary's passport.

At midday, Terry leaves me a final message telling me he's passed on my details to his legal representatives.

*

"You work next door?"

"Yep. I'm the manager."

Or was…

"Wow, you must have seen some stuff there in your time."

Late afternoon, I'm sitting at the bar, drinking tea out of my own mug and reading the paper. An excitable little chap wearing a green beanie hat and builder's boots is at the bar sinking pints of ale. He sets his glass down, nods at Cub for another, turns to me and says, "What's your name?"

*

I open up as usual on Tuesday night. Terry is back in the building. His legal team found a loophole which allowed him to retake control of the place, for the time being at least. Apparently, Ian acted illegally when he took the building back because he should have given Terry two weeks' notice. So, he's also had to give Terry keys for the three main locks that his locksmith changed.

Terry gives me a set of the new keys and tells me that he's sorry for what happened.

"What are you going to do?" I ask.

"I'm thinking London."

He looks slightly skyward when he says it. He always was.

*

A troubled reign is drawing to an end and everybody knows it. The club functions as normal but it's a strange time. We all still have our jobs. Terry and his agents are departing at the end of the week. I hear from Dave Abbott, who's been a close friend of Ian's for years, that after worming his way back into the building, Terry made one last desperate attempt to strike up another lease with Ian under another company name. It would have been the third.

As it stands, things are about to change. A busy lock-in after Cheese Night, all the staff stay, sitting around and looking at me for the answers.

They should know I never had any.

*

Terry writes a long, protracted note which he sticks to the wall behind the bar, giving a rather one-sided view of what happened, announcing that he'll be leaving Munks and saying that on Saturday night, he'll be staying for a drink after work and all the staff are welcome to join him to, as he puts it, 'toast the good memories'.

And every day and night, here, there—sitting at the bar in The Bellhop, standing on the street smoking a cigarette and looking down at the snow on the road, I get dozens of people coming up to me, asking what's happening with Munks. I tell them that all I know is Terry is leaving and Ian is planning to lease the building to someone else. The next king of grime. Hopefully, he'll be taller than Terry. In more ways than one.

*

I get a text from Dave Abbott one afternoon.

What are you up to, mate?
Not much
Fancy a pint?
Yeah
Pick you up in half an hour

*

Dave picks me up in his Clio which is somehow still running, and we go to The Crazy Bear—a pub on the outskirts of the city. He buys us a pint each and we sit in a quiet corner where he tells me that he's going into business with Ian as a fifty-fifty partner.

"And I have a proposition for you…"

He slides a document in front of me—**CONTRACT OF EMPLOYMENT**

The first proper contract for a manager of Munks. A good salary, proper bonuses. I flick to a page and see these words in big bold letters: **THE PRESERVATION OF LIFE SHALL OVERRIDE ALL OTHER CONSIDERATIONS.**

"Have a good think about it, mate."

*

I sit at the bar, drinking a small Rum and Coke, staring at the dotted line where I'm supposed to sign.

*

"Do we know who it is yet?"

We're sitting at the round table after Empire. I've bought everyone a drink.

"As far as I know, someone has come in, at the moment a silent partner, prepared to go in fifty-fifty with Ian."

"So, we still have our jobs then?" asks Blizzie.

"Well, unless they decide to sack us all straightaway."

*

Next door with the Fume and Bret on a Friday lunchtime.

"You know that Dom says he's going to walk out," I say.

"What an idiot," says the Fume.

"Well, I'm encouraging him," I say. "It'll save the new owner a hell of a lot of hassle with severance and redundancy pay."

"Do you know who it is?" asks Bret.

I'm rolling a cigarette. "I do, yes."

"It's Dave Abbott, isn't it?"

I drop my fag. "How do you know that?"

"It doesn't take a genius to work it out."

"That's true."

*

It's the last Desire that Munks will ever see. Just over one hundred come through the door. There's no band on,

Aaron is doing his last gig—he plays whatever the fuck he wants and drinks his usual eight cans of Carling in two hours, then asks for more.

Dom is nowhere to be seen. He and Terry have almost finished clearing out their office.

I sit on the door till, feeling the passport in my pocket, looking up whenever somebody comes in, looking for her face.

*

Nobody stays after work for a drink on Saturday. Terry comes to my office door where I'm taking my time cashing up.

"Everyone's gone," he says.

"Have they?"

"Yes. I was going to thank them all and buy them a drink."

He looks heartbroken.

"I'll have one with you, Terry."

*

After I finish cashing up, I have one drink with him and then make my excuses and go next door. I leave him sitting at the round table, alone, staring at the ground.

*

Monday morning, I watch from my window as Terry turns up in a pickup truck and parks on the double yellow lines on the road outside Munks. He and a young guy, probably his son, load some furniture onto the back—a desk, a filing cabinet, a few boxes, his desk chair that always made him look like a child king. Then he drives off.

*

Another staff meeting. I stand at the back, as usual. All the bouncers are here, even some of the DJs, including Chuchy, who has done his time and is now allowed back in. No sign of Dom, of course, or Georgie—nobody knows what her intentions are now her boyfriend has walked.

Dave Abbott stands at the front, twitches, slightly nervous, excited.

"Erm, alright, guys. As some of you know by now, I have come in, erm, alongside Ian, as his partner, and erm, yeah, bought this place."

"Wow," says Jordan Bone, "Get on, Dave."

"Yes, Dave!" says Chuchy.

"Yeah, an exciting time. Risky, maybe mad—I've had to put my house on this, so it better fucking work or I'm homeless."

There are a few laughs.

"Can you get rid of the mould in the cloakie?" asks Tattoo Paul, "I've had a cough for the last six months."

"Of course, yeah. Once we've cleared all Terry's crap out, the plan is to get some guys in and give this place a bit of love where it needs it. We're going to make it work again, restore Munks back to the place it used to be. Ian is going to remain in the background, and I will be, erm, be the face of the partnership, running the place, with a little help, of course."

He looks at me.

"Are you getting rid of the kitchen?" asks Little Harry.

"Definitely," says Dave. "The plan is to put some sort of shots bar where that is now. At the moment, that room is just a wasted space… but yeah, we have lots of plans. It's going to take time, these things won't happen overnight. We need to build the business back up again, make the most of freshers' week etc., market the place properly, because as you know, the previous owners ran it into the ground and there are a lot of pieces for us to pick up. And hopefully, we'll start getting some big DJs, some big bands back in to play here."

*

What is the worst thing you have ever seen?

*

"Cub… do you know a girl called Henrietta Mary?"

"I don't think so… what does she look like?"

"She wears band t-shirts—Nirvana, Bowie."

"Oh, yeah, Bowie girl. Dirty blonde hair."

"That's her. Do you know her?"

"No, not really, only in passing... and I haven't seen her for a while. She used to come in here with Luke's ex-girlfriend. But yeah, she hasn't come in for ages, which is strange because she used to be here every weekend."

*

Half dark outside early on a Friday morning, and even though I've only just closed the club, there's a party still going on downstairs in The Bellhop, so I have to sneak past them to get to my room where I lock myself away, listening to 'Space Oddity' by Bowie on repeat and loud enough to block it all out, staring out of the window, smoking cigarette after cigarette and wondering if this is her favourite song too.

*

A year in my life according to Facebook:

Kids can watch anything on YouTube these days—He's coming to steal my eyes, to seal my mouth with dirt—I am not what I am—The more you try to erase me—Please don't let me be misunderstood—A guy just paid me £1 for water—Anyone up for a few beers tonight, you know where?—Open When Sober—Some of the things that happen in this place you cannot make up—Man asleep in toilet in his own puke, piss and shit—ANDREW BRANAGH you should be ashamed of yourself—This isn't happening, I'm not here—just fingered myself and got a pooey finger… bad times—I just Facebook raped the fuck out Andrew Branagh—Has anybody seen Freddy Nelson?—People have died in this cloakroom—Tomorrow comes today—See you at the bar—I am the walrus—Exit Music—Ask my demons—Redemption —Sail to the Moon—CHUCHY!—This place is full of pricks—Old man, take a look at my life, I'm a lot like you were—The left eye has gone—god's honest truth im a massive homo—Anyone fancy doing a shift on the doortill tonight at Munks? Will pay cash!—The ruins are no place to play—really fucking need a scarf—What is all this white stuff?—Why do people bare their souls on this reprehensible social networking site?—Rapture—In a little while, I'll be gone—Ground control to Major Tom—Where you runnin' to?—Where you runnin' to?—Let me hold your hand—I FUCK KIDS—Sinnerman, where you gonna run to?

*

I deactivate my Facebook account.

*

"Are you sure about this?"

"Absolutely. I've been here long enough now."

Cheese Night, a night Dave no longer needs to split. 'Heart of Glass' by Blondie is playing in the club, muffled through the office door.

"Well, it's a shame of course, but I respect your decision, mate. What are you planning?"

"I'm not sure—maybe I'll go to uni. I saw a poster advertising a 'Life Direction' course the other day."

He smiles. I laugh.

"Maybe not, eh? Perhaps what I need is a long holiday. One I'm not sure I'll be coming back from."

I hold out a hand.

He takes it.

"It's been good," he says. "You've done a great job here, all these years. In fact, I don't think this place would still be standing if it weren't for you."

I smile again.

"I'll give the Fume my keys tomorrow."

*

I leave the office, walk past the cloakroom where a queue of girls are peeling off their coats, give Tattoo Paul the thumbs up, go to the downstairs bar and watch the Fume and Little Harry and Blizzie serve drinks, ask them if they need any change, bump into Dancing Man by the arch holding his usual two Vodka and Lemonades and staring longingly at the packed dance floor, at the lost girls singing along to 'Holding out for a Hero'. I climb the stairs to check on Bran and Tanya behind the upstairs bar, wink at Blanche who's on her usual stool with her stockinged legs crossed, then go past the door till, past Mike and Sam IDing people on the door, through the groups of smokers—nod to a couple of regulars who have been coming here for years but whose names I have never learnt—and retreat to my usual place in the shadows.

I look up at the stars. Light a cigarette. There is a queue to get in, the first for a long, long time. I search the line for faces. And there, towards the back, standing with a few other girls, I see her. Feel the passport in my pocket. Wait. Watch. Smoke my cigarette. It's definitely her. She is laughing, full-mouthed. She turns and looks up at the tall guy standing behind her, moves her head up slightly to kiss him.

I watch no more. Pull my hood up. Roll another cigarette, smoke it slowly. The queue shifts down and Henrietta Mary goes into the club without seeing me.

My phone vibrates.

A text from Bret saying he started writing the novel today.

I ask him if he has a title yet.

Not yet. But I need stories. Everybody's stories.

And I smile, and type back—*When do you want to meet?* before adding *What am I called?* but I delete the second question before I press send because I realise that I already know the answer.

I have no name. I need no name. Because I don't really exist—not in a place like this, where it is all too easy to disappear entirely. Because everybody here wants to be somewhere else. Because everybody here is an imposter.

The End

Acknowledgments

… I need stories. Everybody's stories.

Lot's of people have been instrumental in the creation of this novel. Without your help, this story could never have been told. This list is not exhaustive, and I apologise if I've left anyone out: Craig Stock, Gaby Lawbuary-Stock, Anthony Prothero, Andy Hales, Mush Lusher, Spencer Harrison-Page, Stacie Lee, Tom Maddicott, Kelvin Swaby, Tom Chambers, James Murray, Stephen O'Neil, Joseph Sudell, Joseph Batten, Ollie Love.

Thanks to Stew Foster and Jonathan Bentley-Smith for the many days spent in The (real) Bellhop, nursing one pint for three hours, our manuscripts on the table in front of us covered in red pen.

Above all, I'd like to thank my family, especially Una Grose for being my first reader, all those years ago.

And finally, thanks to my partner, Emily Rose, for convincing me to dig this novel out from its 10 year hibernation, and helping me to bring it into the world. Without this wonderful woman's support, you would not be holding this book in your hands.

BG
6.9.2022

Printed in Great Britain
by Amazon

13916374R00171